The Winning of Opie

The Winning of Opie

DICK FLEMING

DOUBLEDAY & COMPANY, INC.

GARDEN CITY, NEW YORK

1978

For
Jeanne Williams
who
gave me a kick

All of the characters in this book are fictitious,
and any resemblance to actual persons, living or dead,
is purely coincidental.

First Edition
ISBN: 0-385-14467-9
Library of Congress Catalog Card Number 78-7753
Copyright © 1978 by Richard Jarvis Fleming
All Rights Reserved
Printed in the United States of America

Chapter 1

Doc Killian had a full house. Not in cards, but in company. Five men had answered his invitation to play poker. They were all seated around the big kitchen table in Doc's house, each man studying his cards. It had been three years since last they had played cards together. What had once been a weekly meeting was now a reunion.

Doc hurriedly glanced around the circle of men. A general feeling of uneasiness was reflected in the stiffness with which they sat in the high-backed chairs. It was as though each man was on his guard and sat poised on the edge of his chair ready to spring into action at a signal from Doc. They didn't sprawl loosely as men generally do in a friendly card game. They kept both feet planted squarely on the floor and cast little flickering glances at each other out of the corners of their eyes.

Hell! They were all uneasy. Doc himself was. His long surgeon's fingers gripped his cards as though he never intended to turn them loose.

It hadn't been that way in the old days. Doc released his grip and shifted the cards in his hands. These six men had once been accustomed to meeting here in Doc's kitchen for a relaxed, informal, jovial, joshing, weekly game of cards that merely served as a pretense for them to enjoy each other's company.

But that was a long time ago. Three years back, before Doc had been framed and sent to the Arizona Territorial Prison at Yuma for a crime he hadn't committed. And now he was back.

The first thing Doc had done since returning from prison was to set a meeting of the old weekly poker club. Wouldn't a man who had been gone for three years want to see his old friends? Supposedly they were still his friends. Yet things and people change. Old friends change in their attitudes towards a man. Especially when he's been to prison.

Doc stared at his hand, but his mind was scanning the other players. Big Bill McClure, the blacksmith, was a mountain of a man. He stood six feet six inches tall, weighed in the neighborhood of three hundred pounds, and not an ounce of that weight was fat. He could pick up a horse and turn the animal over if he had a mind to, and sometimes he did. Well, a small horse anyway.

Bill was a gentle soul. He was the kind of man who never got mad, or upset, or in a hurry. His great strength was kept in check by his easygoing personality.

"Hey, Doc"—the giant's eyes twinkled—"are you dealing or dreaming? How about two more cards?"

Doc unlimbered his long legs and dealt two new cards while Bill threw his discards in the pot. The new cards disappeared behind Bill's big hands. Slowly he shuffled them around until he finally found a combination that pleased him. Then he folded the card hand against his barrel chest and sat watching the flame of the kerosene lamp that stood on the edge of the round table.

Next to Bill was Amos Dalton, the sheriff. He was a whipcord of a man. Tall, thin, deadly with a gun. Unlike a lot of gunslingers, Amos hardly ever pulled his weapon. He had a manner about him that cowed ordinary men and made strong bad men hesitate before crossing him. Those few who had gotten over their moment of hesitation never lived to regret it.

For all of that, Amos wasn't a cold-blooded killer. He was a man sensitive to the moods of other people. This trait was what made him a good sheriff. He could handle an unruly drunk, a hysterical woman, an irate citizen, or a lynch mob with equal facility.

"If I was as slow on the draw as you are at drawing cards, Doc, I'd a been dead long ago," said Amos. "Give me one more card."

Doc flipped Amos the card but knew by the expression on his thin face that it wasn't the high card he had expected.

Bob Noel sat on the other side of Amos. Bob Noel, the banker. Straight-laced, upright pillar of the community, conservatively dressed, every inch the big money man. Bob was a West Virginia hillbilly in origin and a self-made man in the banking circles of the West.

He'd left the mountains of his native state at the close of the war. He came out to Arizona Territory driving a team of ex-army mules that pulled an ex-army wagon loaded down with ex-army rifles and ammunition.

No one ever asked him where he got the mules, wagon, and guns. Bob never volunteered any information about his worldly possessions. He sold the rifles and ammunition to the settlers on the frontier. He traded the mules and wagon for a building lot on the main street of the town called Gila Crossing. He used his gun profits to build a false-front bank building and started being a banker. He had done well.

His was the only bank between Tucson and Phoenix. He loaned money, foreclosed a few mortgages, bought quite a bit of land, and wound up owning half the town.

But he was a fair man. He helped widows and orphans and ranchers who were down on their luck. He promoted the economic life of his town. He was a great booster of local trade. People liked him. Even though he was the richest man in the community and most of the townspeople were poor, he certainly never lost his common touch.

"Man," chuckled Bob, adjusting his diamond stickpin, "you're the most tight-fisted dealer I ever saw in a card game. If I had you working for me at the bank, I wouldn't ever have to worry about you lending too much of my money. I need two."

As Doc peeled off the two cards he sensed that Bob didn't need the extra pasteboards. He was just playing the percentage chance.

Next came Jim Balinte, undertaker by profession, philosopher by choice. Short of stature, well fleshed out, he sported a mustache and goatee that made him a distinguished-looking figure of a man.

Jim had been a Hungarian cavalryman who emigrated to the States in time to help Sherman make his sweep through Georgia. His cavalry troop had followed him through all the major engagements with the Confederacy and would have rode with him through hell. He was the kind of natural leader who instilled devotion in his followers and love in the hearts of his friends.

At the close of the war he was mustered out at Savannah, Georgia. Not having any ties left in the land of his birth, or any reason to stay in the East, he rode across the country to Arizona Territory and settled in Gila Crossing.

There, because of his innate gentility and because he was the kind of man to whom people turned in their hour of need, he became the town mortician and resident philosopher.

"If you don't mind, Doc"—Balinte crossed his short arms over his potbelly—"I'll just fold for this hand. The wise man awaits a better opportunity."

Doc passed a hand through his long, gray hair as he sucked in his slight paunch so he could sit up closer to the table.

Finally there was Bryce Collins, the owner of the livery stable. Bryce was the youngest of the five men. Handsome, with piercing gray-green eyes, an athlete's body, and long, wavy hair; Bryce was intelligent, a good time companion, and a prankster whose practical jokes often kept the group in stitches.

Bryce had a way with women. His youthful exuberance and gift of gab had turned the head of many a female. Women just naturally went out of their way to get themselves in compromising situations with Bryce.

It was a kind of game with him, this dazzling of females. He was so full of animal magnetism that any woman would feel slighted if he didn't make some effort to amuse and confuse her.

There was a story current in Gila Crossing about Bryce and a girl named Vicki. She had come to town to live with some cousins. She and Bryce started attending affairs around town and going for long buggy rides in the surrounding countryside. Gossip had it that they were going to get married.

One day Vicki up and married another man. About eight months later she presented her new husband with a child. There was a lot of talk about how much the child resembled Bryce. The funny thing about the whole affair was that Bryce and Vicki and Vick's new husband remained the best of friends.

"I'll stand pat." Bryce patted his cards against the table. "I never did like to break up a winning hand by drawing more cards. Now, if you amateur card sharks will ante up a little more of your loose change, I'll show you what a straight flush looks like."

Doc's hands tensed on his own cards. Pure bluff. But Bryce's attractiveness was no sham. With him around, a man had better keep close tabs on his wife.

And that reminded Doc of his wife, Jeanne. Doc had met her when he first came to Gila Crossing and hung out his shingle to practice medicine.

Jeanne had come into Doc's office, which was located in a storefront on the main street of Gila Crossing. She had complained that her right leg pained her. Doc had examined the leg, minutely, but couldn't find a thing the matter with it. He had also examined her left leg. Finally he admitted that they were the best-looking pair of legs he had ever seen on a woman, but there didn't seem to be any medical problem. Jeanne had laughed and said the problem was getting a doctor to notice you when you were perfectly healthy. Then they had both laughed together.

Doc had found in Jeanne that elusive quality that he'd always sought in a woman. She was youth, lost dreams, manhood's fantasies, and loveliness. But above all she was intelligent. Finding a woman whose intellect matched his, Doc had fallen hopelessly in love with Jeanne and mooned over her like a love-sick schoolboy. He was forty-four years old at the time.

Physically Jeanne was a small woman. She stood five feet two inches tall. Had lovely chestnut colored hair. Deep brown eyes that formed limpid pools of merriment. Pert, firm young breasts, a boyishly supple body and perfect legs. There was an air of poise and confidence about her.

She was the kind of woman who could enter a room full of strangers and in five minutes have every man present hanging on her every word. Other women felt old and frumpy in her presence. But the simple friendliness of her basic personality made those same women like her.

Altogether she was a beautiful woman, and all woman. She also had a certain set to her jaw that had made Doc wonder just how stubborn she could be when the need arose. Later on in their married life he found out she could be obstinate. Jeanne had a streak of stubbornness in her that could drive a man, especially a husband, to distraction.

Theirs was a story-book romance. A whirlwind courtship that ended in a perfectly proper marriage ceremony. The whole town had attended their wedding. After a brief honeymoon, spent in Tucson, the newlyweds set up housekeeping in Gila Crossing.

Jeanne's wedding present to Doc had been a gun. It was a special gun. He had long wanted a pocket double derringer. This gun was made by Remington Arms from an Elliot design. It was first patented in 1865, had a bird's-head grip, was a cartridge-firing two-shot .41 rimfire with over/under barrels. Just the sort of pocket gun a professional man would want to carry.

Doc's wedding present to Jeanne had been a new house. For the time and place it was a good house. It had the usual front parlor for company. Two upstairs bedrooms. A separate ground floor room for Doc's office. A formal dining room and a large kitchen. The kitchen was the center of activity in the house. In the kitchen area Doc had installed a large, round, expandable, kitchen table on which ordinary meals were taken.

This table had also become the scene of weekly poker games that, next to Jeanne, had been Doc's ruling passion. Here he had invited his friends to help him indulge in the one game of skill and chance that knows no social barriers.

Jeanne had been the perfect hostess. During the weekly

poker games she had kept the players supplied with coffee and sandwiches. She had also entered into the good-natured raillery of the company of men. Often, as Jeanne had fulfilled her duties as hostess, Doc had looked at her with pride and thankfulness that destiny had caused their meeting.

They had enjoyed three years of connubial bliss and then Jeanne was dead. During that time she had made Doc reach the heights of ecstasy and the depths of despair. She could be an angel one moment and a devil the next. He never really completely understood her. And that was part of the fatal fascination she had for him.

Sometimes he had wanted to wring her neck. But always, above all else, he loved her. Loved her with the single-minded devotion of a man who had found the one woman who could make his life complete.

When Jeanne died, Doc's life had crumbled into little pieces. Bits so small that he could not gather them up again. He had felt as though he too had been broken. His reason for living gone. Even now that he was free, in a way, it was worse to be home, in a house he had shared with Jeanne.

Doc came out of his reverie and examined his own hand. He was surprised to find he'd dealt himself four aces and a deuce. This was the first game he had dealt in three years. That is, a real game. You could hardly count the many games he had played in prison with matches for stakes. He was glad to see this omen of good luck. He needed it.

"Come on, Doc." Bryce flashed a brilliant smile at him. "Are you going to drop out or stay and play with the men?"

"I'll stay," said Doc. "I won't need any more cards to beat a four flusher like you."

"That's how I like to hear you talk, Doctor. I'm aiming to do me a little operation on your wallet. After all, it isn't every night I get a chance to do surgery on a cutup like you."

Doc considered the odds. With Jim folded, Amos asking for one card, Bob calling for two, Bill going for two, and Bryce running a flush bluff; chances are he had them all beat. If Bryce was really bluffing.

"O.K., Brycey Boy. Get some money on the table and we'll find out who the men are."

Bryce looked like a cherub with a secret. "Bet you a buck I've got a straight flush."

"I'll fold." Amos' thin lips closed on his words.

"Gentlemen, I'll see you," blustered Bob.

Jim settled his round bottom more firmly in his chair. "This is my night for meditation, not card playing."

"Can't stand this exalted company," said Bill. "Not on the crummy cards you just gave me." His big hands smashed the cards together and he slammed them down on the table.

Doc flipped his dollar into the pot. "Let's see what you got, boys."

Bob turned over a full house. Bryce really did have a straight flush.

"It's always a pleasure to lose money to your friends," Doc shrugged as he turned up his four aces and a deuce.

Bryce raked in his winnings and Bill started the shuffle for the next deal. Doc let the cards pile up in front of him as he looked from one man to another. None of them would meet his gaze. They were all determinedly busy sorting their cards.

Damn them! Doc ground his teeth together in impotent rage. One of them was guilty of murdering his wife. Doc was determined to find out who the guilty party was—and kill him. The only problem was he didn't know which one.

Chapter 2

Doc's mind drifted back to that night, three years before, when Jeanne had died.

It had been a lush spring night in Arizona. There had been an unusual amount of rain that season and the desert had bloomed with wild flowers. Brief spots of beauty that lived their small hour in the sun and faded away to nothingness. Even as Jeanne had done.

The Noels had held a garden party that night. All the prominent members of Gila Crossing high society had attended. There was music and dancing, food and drink, quiet conversation, boisterous hijinks—and death!

Jeanne had been at her loveliest. She had worn a simple pale-blue dress that had small mirrorlike pieces of metal sewn on its front in a butterfly pattern. As she moved, walked, talked, and danced, her dress had reflected the light in a pattern that matched her sparkling personality. As usual, she'd had more dancing partners on her program than she had room to note. Doc had been hard pressed to get every fourth dance with his wife.

There had been a large punch bowl on the refreshment table filled with a delectable wine punch that held a considerable punch. It was being served by Opal Johnson, the schoolteacher. Caught up in the gaiety of the moment, Doc had visited the punch bowl more than his usual allotment and was feeling no pain.

"Ain't I seen you a time or two tonight, Sonny?" Opal had asked as Doc held out his glass for a refill.

Opal hadn't looked very schoolteacherish to Doc at that moment. In fact, for a schoolma'am she'd looked downright pretty. Her light brown hair, which was usually swept back in a ponytail, had been let down for the evening and its soft looseness shimmered in the lamplight. The long dress she wore hid the thinness of her tall body. Even her glasses were less noticeable than usual. The thought had come to Doc that Opal was wearing entirely different clothing, hair style, and glasses than she did in her usual role of schoolteacher.

"Don't believe you have," Doc had grinned at the punch bowl custodian. "You see before you, madam, a new and different man each time he comes into your domain. I was a doctor name of Killian when first you saw me. But now I have progressed through various stages into other men and other forms until you now behold a man fast turning himself into a jackass."

Opal had smiled, and Doc had been warmed by the appreciation of his little joke that he saw in her eyes.

"Don't go overboard on your magic act just yet, Doc," Opal had said. "Maybe you better let your cup dry up and pay a little more attention to what's going on at this party. For one thing, your wife has been gone from this room for a spell, and for another, so have all of your men friends."

Now what had she meant by that? Had she thought he was so drunk he couldn't see straight?

"Thanks for the advice, Opal," he'd replied. "I think you've got a point there." Doc had then walked away from the punch bowl and looked around for Jeanne.

She had no longer been in the ballroom. And neither had any of the five men whom he considered his best friends.

He had left the party and started down the long central hallway that led to the library. He'd paused for a moment and looked into the drawing room that was next down the hallway. Jeanne had not been there. Where could she have been? He'd continued to the next room, which was a small sitting room. Jeanne had not been there either.

As Doc had stepped back into the hallway he'd heard the

sound of a muffled shot. It had come from behind the library door at the end of the hallway. A terrible premonition had swept over him. He'd stood frozen as his mind raced. That shot . . . Jeanne's disappearance. Icy fingers had seemed to clutch at his heart, which had begun to pump wildly.

Please, God. Don't let anything happen to Jeanne!

Breaking into a run Doc had covered the distance to the library door. Grasping the massive brass handle he'd shoved open the door. And there he had found her. Crumpled into a small, hurt bundle, he had found her.

Jeanne had lain beautiful in death as she had been in life, except for the gaping, oozing, red, small bullet hole over her heart. Her blood had seeped out, staining the mirrored butterfly pattern of her dress into a grotesque, obscene vision that would haunt Doc for the rest of his life.

There had been a gun next to the body. A small double-barreled derringer. Smoke still curled from its barrel. Doc's punch-befuddled brain had refused to accept the reality. Instinctively he'd reached for Jeanne's wrist seeking her pulse. There had been none. He'd gently lifted an eyelid. The blankness of death had looked out at him.

He'd stared at Jeanne in shock and numbness. All of his medical training had been gone as naught. No power in his surgeon's hands to reverse the irreversible. Jeanne had been gone. Beyond his power to heal.

Blindly he had reached for the gun. The touch of the gun metal had brought some semblance of sanity as he had recognized it was his gun! The one Jeanne had given him for a wedding present. He had cried out. A fierce animal scream that had rended the air stilling the music and babble of voices at the other end of the house.

Doc had still been crouched over Jeanne when Sheriff Dalton ran into the library.

"Doc!" Amos had shouted. "What in hell's going on here?"

"Jeanne," was all that Doc could mumble. He had pointed at her body with his hand that still held the gun.

Amos had stepped over Jeanne's body and felt for a pulse at her wrist. Then he'd straightened up and took a long, hard look at Doc. Slowly he had reached over and taken the gun out of Doc's hand.

"Did you do it?" he had asked.

"I didn't—I couldn't—" Slow, hard sobs had wracked Doc's body.

He'd buried his face in his hands, trying to blot out what had happened. Soon the other guests had crowded into the library, hushing as they saw Jeanne's body. Doc had opened his eyes to face curious stares. They were all his friends, but he had noticed a wariness in the looks they had given him.

"I didn't do it!" Doc had shouted. He hadn't been able to believe the dreadful truth. He had needed help, comfort. Instead. . . . Swallowing, he had almost hated the shocked people who seemed to fill the room. "I loved her! It wasn't me," he had tried to tell them. There had been no movement, no other sound in the room. Nothing but awed silence.

Only one pair of eyes had looked at him with more compassion than curiosity. Opal Johnson had made as though to reach out to him, but Doc spun from her and caught Amos by the shoulders.

"Don't just stand there!" Doc had flung at Amos. "Find whoever did it. He may be getting away."

Amos had tried to shake Doc off, but enraged, Doc had gripped the sheriff tighter.

"Damn you!" he'd cried. "Who killed her? Help me catch whoever killed her!"

Strong arms had grappled with Doc, finally dragged him off Amos. Big Bill had put a hammerlock on Doc's right arm, and Amos, his left. The three men had surged into the crowd, knocking people about like nine pins going down before a bowler's ball, till at last, Doc had gone down.

"All right," Amos had said. "Let's get him out of here. I'll lock him up for safekeeping until he calms down and can tell us what happened. Help me with him, Bill. Jim, look after the body."

Doc had tried to crawl back over to Jeanne, reach her one last time, but the two men wrestled him down the hallway, outside to the dusty street.

"Find the killer!" Doc had sobbed as Amos put him into a jail cell and locked the door. "Lock me up, but for God's sake get out and look around!! There must be some sign! Don't let him get away!"

Amos had looked at him with pity in his eyes. "I'm sorry to have to lock you up, Doc," he'd said. "But there's a lot of circumstantial evidence here that says I have to put you under arrest. I hate to think it of you, but all I know is what I've seen with my own eyes."

"Amos, listen—"

The sheriff's eyes had flashed. "You're not yourself right now. This is a terrible shock to all of us and to you more than anyone. Why don't you try to get some sleep and we'll talk about it tomorrow."

Turning on his heel, the sheriff had walked out with his helper and left Doc alone with his grief, the loss he still couldn't believe; and the terrible knowledge that while his friend, the sheriff, thought he was doing him a favor by locking him up, Jeanne's killer was getting away.

Chapter 3

A coroner's jury, led by Jim Balinte, held an inquest the next day. Their verdict: "Deceased met her death as the result of a .41 caliber bullet fired at close range into the heart. Death was instantaneous. Evidence presented at the inquest indicates that the felony of murder has been committed. It is the charge of this jury that an indictment be returned against Dr. V. A. Killian for this crime."

Doc received word of the inquest's findings in his jail cell. He was still in a state of shock. His numbed mind could hardly recognize what was being said to him.

He grabbed the messenger's arm and shook him. "Listen to me! It doesn't matter what those fools on the coroner's jury report. Tell Amos that he's got to find Jeanne's killer. I didn't do it. While all this talking and investigating is going on the killer's getting away. For God's sake, man, do something!"

The man twisted away from Doc's clutching hands. "Don't take it out on me, Doc. I just came over to let you know what's going on." The man hurried away.

Hopeless! No one would listen to him. Doc lay back down on the cell bunk and stared open-eyed at the ceiling. As the receding footsteps of the news bearer echoed down the hallway of the jail, Doc's soul cried out in anguish: *Jeanne, Jeanne, Jeanne.*

Later on that day, Amos, Bill, Bryce, Jim, and Bob had come to see Doc in a group. Amos acted as spokesman for them all.

"Doc, we're all sorry as can be about what's happened. Can you tell us now what you know about Jeanne's death?"

Doc shrugged his shoulders. "Not much to tell, boys. I heard a shot. When I got to the library, Jeanne was already dead."

The five friends exchanged glances. "But what about the gun?" Amos pursued. "When I came in you were holding it in your hand—and it was still smoking."

"I made an honest mistake, Amos. When I saw my gun lying beside Jeanne, I picked it up. I shouldn't have done that. I don't know why I did it. Just sort of a reflex action."

The five men shifted positions uneasily. "But don't you see," continued Amos, "there's some pretty strong circumstantial evidence against you in this case. We'd all like to help you if we can. But what can we say against the evidence?"

Doc pondered his answer. "I appreciate your concern, fellows. All I can tell you is I didn't do it."

"How about some evidence to prove your point?" Amos went on. "Did you notice anybody else being in the library when you first came in?"

"I didn't see any sign of anyone being there," said Doc. "Of course I'll admit I kind of lost my head. My main concern was Jeanne. Maybe I wasn't looking too well, but I'm sure somebody must have come in, killed Jeanne, and left before I arrived."

"That's going to be hard to prove," said Amos.

Doc nodded grimly. Then the five men shook Doc's hand, assured him they would keep their ears and eyes open, and before they left, once again offered their condolences over his wife's death.

During the time he was locked up, Doc had only one other visitor besides his friends. One day Opal Johnson came to see him. The jailer would not let her go into his cell. She stood in the hallway just outside the bars.

"Buck up," said Opal. Her light blue eyes were soft, full of concern. "It's not the end of the world yet."

Doc couldn't speak. The kindness of this woman in coming to see him in his hour of need touched him as few other things had. He tried to make answer, but no words would come.

"Doc, is there anything I can do?"

He mutely shook his head. A woman couldn't track down a cold-blooded killer. That was Amos' job. "Go home," Doc said roughly. "Don't come back. It won't do me any good and I don't want you involved in my troubles."

Opal whirled and fled down the hallway. He'd hurt, shocked her. But he didn't want her ostracized for visiting him.

Doc sank back down on his bunk.

Shortly thereafter, Doc was taken before the magistrate court judge of Gila Crossing. Magistrate court was held in the county courthouse.

The courthouse was brand spanking new. A monument to a frontier people's belief in law and order, it was made of red brick and cut limestone. Three stories high, surmounted by a handsome cupola from whose windowed viewpoints the citizens of Piñon County could view a sizable segment of their county, the courthouse stood rock firm and imposing amid the desert wastes of Arizona Territory. Wide, keystoned arches framed the front entryway.

Doc was led, handcuffed, through the main door, down the long, first-floor hallway, and then up the wide steps of a curved stairway to the second-floor courtroom. Judge Easley was presiding.

The high judge's bench commanded the front of the room. A wooden railing separated the bench from the rest of the courtroom. Rows of chairs were tiered throughout the rest of the chamber, so interested citizens could have an uninterrupted view of the proceedings. There was a large audience present for Doc's arraignment. Many of the people had come from out of town, lured by the excitement of a murder trial. Many strange faces filled the courtroom.

"Doctor Killian"—the judge's sepulchral voice floated through the court chamber—"you are charged with the felony of first-degree murder in the death of your late wife, Jeanne Killian. How do you plead?"

Doc stood silently before the bench, felt waves of outrage and condemnation striking him so intensely that he felt as if he were being lacerated by the blows of a blacksnake whip.

"He's guilty as hell!" cried a voice from the rear.

"You're wasting time, Judge. Hang him!" yelled another voice.

"Let's get a rope!" sounded still another.

"Order—order in the court." Judge Easley rapped his gavel. "If there are any further outbursts I will have this court cleared. Bailiff, eject the next man who speaks out of turn."

A babble of voices muttered and groused for a few moments, then stilled as the judge continued. "And now, if we may proceed? Prisoner, you have heard the charge, how do you plead? Guilty or not guilty?"

Doc swallowed the lump that threatened to choke him. "Not guilty!" he flung out.

A hubbub broke out. Men sprang from their seats pressing forward as if to seize the prisoner. The bailiff was hard put to restore order.

Banging his gavel furiously the judge shouted: "Silence in the court! Certain forms must be observed and I intend to see the letter of the law followed here. This man is innocent until proven guilty and I will hold any man who says otherwise in contempt of court."

Judge Easley glared down at the audience for a moment and then turned to Doc. "Prisoner at the bar, you are hereby remanded into the custody of the sheriff of Piñon County, to be held without bail, until such time as the circuit court shall meet to consider your case. Court adjourned."

The angry crowd jumped to its feet hurling abuse and threats at Doc as Amos led him out a side entrance and returned him to his cell.

"Don't pay any attention to those hotheads," said Amos as he locked the cell door. "Most of the loudest ones were half drunk. I'm going to see that the saloon is closed down the day you have to go to circuit court."

"I'd appreciate that, Amos."

Left alone in the lockup, Doc paced up and down and considered his position. Charged with a murder he hadn't committed! Rage at the injustice of the charge made him stop and pound his fists against the wall. The pain this caused in his knuckles made him sit down and try to think calmly about his predicament.

Doc sucked at the blood from his abraded hands. His good sense told him how his case must appear to others. He had been found, with a still-smoking gun in his hand, standing over the body of his dead wife. In the absence of any other logical suspect, he was number one. Doc knew he hadn't killed Jeanne. Then who had?

For the first time he made a methodical effort to reconstruct the scene of the crime. He had been at the punch bowl getting himself another drink (one too many perhaps?). As he noticed his wife was missing from the room his eyes had continued to sweep the assembly. Subconsciously his brain had registered the fact of his five friends also being absent.

Where had they been? Why were all five of them gone at the same time he missed Jeanne? Could one of them have been the murderer?

But why? What possible motive could any of these men have for killing a woman who had never done them any harm, a woman apparently well liked by them all? Was there something in Jeanne's past that might have led to the murder?

And then he forced himself to remember in detail what had met his eyes when he entered the library. Jeanne on the floor. Smoking gun next to her body as though dropped in the haste of flight. The tall, double french doors leading to the back garden were ajar. There had been no sign of a struggle. No furniture was overturned or anything out of place. It was as though someone had passed swiftly through the doors, shot Jeanne, and then as swiftly vanished. It didn't make sense. But it had happened.

Then Doc thought about his five friends. Up to this point he would have trusted any of them with his life or his wife. Had he been blind to what should have been obvious?

Had his wife been unfaithful to him—with one of his friends? No! His stomach muscles tensed. He felt nauseated. That was impossible! Jeanne hadn't been that kind of a woman. She had been too open and honest. Surely if something like that had been going on she herself would have come to him and told him the truth.

Or would she? Doc shut his eyes and tried to deny that such a thing could have been, fought to hold onto his love. Damn these people who were driving him crazy, making him even dream such madness! If Amos was doing his job, the murderer might be in this cell, facing what he deserved.

Jeanne loved me. Whyever she died, she loved me. Doc clung to that.

But the doubts remained. And they were worse than the threat of execution.

Doc languished in jail for two months before the next session of the circuit court was held. Once again he was taken from his jail cell and made the long march through the courthouse entryway, down the long hall, up the stairs to the courtroom.

"Hear ye, hear ye, hear ye," the bailiff's stentorian voice rang out. "The Circuit Court of Piñon County, Arizona Territory, the Honorable Judge Thurman presiding, is now in session. The court will please rise."

All present rose as the judge entered the chamber, took his place on the bench, rapped with his gavel, and settled back to hear the case. The jury was in place and the courtroom was packed with a capacity crowd.

The first witness to be called was Sheriff Amos Dalton. He was sworn and gave his testimony.

The sheriff told about how on the night of the killing he was standing outside the Noel house on the front porch talking to his deputy, Sid Harris, when he heard Doc give a yell. He said he had run through the house and found Doc standing over his dead wife's body with a gun in his hand.

Sheriff Dalton identified the gun as being a .41 caliber derringer and that it was a gun known to belong to Doc.

He stated that it had taken him less than one minute to reach the library from the time he had heard Doc yell and that he had seen no one else at the scene of the crime except Doc.

"There was no sign of anyone else having been in the library," said the sheriff. "After I locked Doc up in the jail that night I doubled back to the scene of the crime and very carefully checked for evidence. There was no sign of a struggle in the library. I couldn't find anyone at the party who had seen a stranger come and go. Doc's the only man I can place at the scene of the crime when it happened."

The second witness to be called was Jim Balinte, the coroner. His testimony told of how he had been out in the kitchen of the Noel house getting some paprika to spice up his drink when he had heard Doc's cry. He estimated that Jeanne had been dead about five minutes before his own arrival in the library. Balinte also said that he had not seen any other logical suspects except for Doc in the vicinity of the dead woman. The coroner was asked for his expert opinion as to the cause of Jeanne's death. He replied that she had been killed by a .41 caliber bullet that was probably fired from Doc's gun.

"There was no other gun at the scene of the crime," Balinte said. "Whether or not Doc pulled the trigger is something for the jury to decide, not me."

Bob Noel was called to the stand and replied under questioning that Doc's wife had been younger than he and had been known to have other male friends before Doc came on the scene. He further stated that Doc's wife had been the belle of the ball and danced every dance, not necessarily with her husband. Over the objections of the defense attorney he was led to venture his opinion that perhaps Doc had followed his wife into the library and killed her in a drunken, jealous rage.

"I don't like to think such a thing about a man with Doc's background," Noel explained. "But what else would explain the fact that he was found standing over her dead body with a gun in his hand?"

Opal Johnson reluctantly testified that Doc had consumed too much punch the night of the party and had appeared more than slightly intoxicated to her. She also said that Doc's wife appeared to be flirting with some of the men she had danced with that night. Opal concluded her testimony by saying she didn't think Doc had killed his wife.

Big Bill McClure blundered into a forensic trap laid by the prosecutor and grudgingly spoke of his belief that Doc might have accidentally killed his wife during a quarrel over her flirtatious activities at the party.

"I don't think Doc did it," Bill spoke softly. "But if he did, it must have been an accident."

Bryce Collins admitted that he was one of the many younger men who had danced with Doc's wife during the party. He said that she might have seemed to be flirting with other men but that was just her easygoing manner with men and that he didn't think it should be taken seriously.

"She was a young and pretty woman," said Bryce. "She liked to dance and have a good time. Maybe Doc got a little too drunk and took her actions the wrong way. I hope for his sake he didn't kill her over it."

Other witnesses were produced who confirmed the previous testimony and told how Doc had abruptly left the ballroom and how he had appeared angry as he exited.

During the testimony of these witnesses, Doc seethed inwardly. His hands gripped the arms of his chair and it was all he could do to keep from leaping up and assaulting the witnesses. The injustice of it all! Instead of making some effort to find the real killer, they were condemning him on purely circumstantial evidence. Doc gritted his teeth.

When Doc was finally called to the witness stand, he had recovered from his initial shock at the trend of events. But by then it seemed to him that everyone in town believed he had killed his wife. As his time in jail had lengthened, he noticed that his five friends came to visit him less often. And when they did come, he noticed that a decided chill had set in on their former friendliness. Little flickers of doubt seemed to dot their conversation as they told him no other suspects had been turned up. Well, he couldn't really blame them for what they were thinking.

He felt alone. Defenseless. Locked up like an animal in a cage. It was enough to shake the sanity of any man. It was also the most traumatic of experiences to find that the pack had turned upon him. It was him against the world. Doc did not feel as if he wanted to be a part of that world any longer. But his need to find out the truth, his will to revenge his wife's killing made him surly and antagonistic to the legal process that was stifling his freedom of movement to find the real killer. Doc didn't much care about the outcome of the trial. He lived only for the moment of his revenge.

The bailiff said: "Please raise your right hand."

Doc sat in the witness stand and did not move. A disbelieving murmur swept the crowded courtroom.

The bailiff tried again. "Please raise your right hand and repeat after me."

Still Doc sat mute and unmoving. He didn't care what the legal eagles did. His thoughts were bent on pursuit of the real killer.

Turning to the bench, the bailiff, shrugging, appealed to the judge.

Judge Thurman said: "Will the opposing counsels please approach the bench."

"What in hell's the matter with Doc?" asked Judge Thurman.

"I think he's gone off his rocker, your honor," replied the prosecutor.

"No, your honor, it goes deeper than that," explained the defense attorney. "Doc knows he's innocent of the charge. But since public opinion has turned against him, he doesn't feel there is any point in making a defense."

"Hah! That's what they all say," snorted the prosecutor.

"It's true," rejoined the defense attorney. "All I could get out of Doc when I talked with him in jail was that he was innocent. He told me that if his word wasn't good enough then he didn't intend to offer any defense. He's a proud man and he's been badly hurt by all this."

"We'll see how much pride he's got when I get him at the end of a rope," sneered the prosecutor.

"All right, boys, let's hold it right there," said Judge Thurman. "If he won't speak in his own defense, then this is going to be a mighty short trial. Let me try to talk him into saying something."

The two lawyers went back to their places and the judge addressed Doc. "Defendant at the bar, you have been charged with a crime, the punishment for which is death or life imprisonment. If you have something to say—now is the time to speak your piece."

"I have nothing to say," Doc broke his silence. "Except that I'm not guilty. This whole trial is a farce. Why isn't someone out looking for the real killer instead of blaming me?" Doc's temper brought the blood boiling to his face. He jumped up in the witness stand and raised his fist at the courtroom crowd.

"And all you yahoots out there hankering for my blood!" he shouted at them while shaking his fist. "What are any of you doing to see that justice is done? Have any of you high-spirited citizens been to see the sheriff about finding out if there are any real clues as to who killed my wife?" He stared angrily at the gaping faces. No man's eyes met his.

"I'm disgusted with all of you," Doc spit on the floor to show his contempt. "Not one of you has really tried to help me or even listen to my side of the story. I don't need your help anyway. Somehow, someday, someway, I'm going to get out of this mess and find out who killed Jeanne. And when I do—" he paused and shifted his gaze from face to face, "I'm not going to need the help of gutless wonders like you or any court to see that I get justice." Doc turned his back on the crowd and sat back down in the witness chair.

There was a stunned silence in the courtroom. All eyes appealed to the judge for an answer to Doc's outburst.

"Is that all you have to say in your defense?" asked Judge Thurman.

Doc didn't even look up at the judge.

"Very well then," said Judge Thurman. "Are there any further arguments from counsel?"

The prosecutor got up in front of the jury and went over all the evidence again and pointed out how no other suspect had been found for the murder except Doc. He repeated the serious nature of the crime and admonished the jury to find the defendant guilty of murder in the first degree.

The defense attorney, in his turn, pointed out to the jury that all the evidence presented had been circumstantial in nature, that no one actually saw Doc commit the crime, that they were duty-bound to give him the last benefit of the doubt, and that if they couldn't see their way clear to free him of the charges, the least they could do would be to convict him of second-degree murder, unpremeditated.

"The prisoner will step down," ordered the judge.

Puzzled expressions lit the faces of the audience and the jury. People spoke to one another in subdued but excited whispers. Doc stomped out of the witness stand and resumed his seat at the defense table.

Judge Thurman cleared his throat. "Gentlemen of the jury. You have heard the evidence presented in this court. You have also heard the defendant's testimony, such as it was. You may now retire to consider your verdict."

The jury rose and filed out of the courtroom. The audience sat quietly for a moment and then, in small groups, continued to argue the case among themselves. They did not have long to wonder as to what the verdict would be. In less than fifteen minutes the jury returned.

"Have you reached your verdict?" asked the judge.

"Yes, your honor, we have," said the jury foreman. "We find the defendant guilty of murder—in the second degree."

"That's not the right answer!" yelled a voice from the crowd.

"Let's string him up!" came another.

Judge Thurman gaveled down the disturbance. "The prisoner will approach the bench."

Doc and the defense attorney went up before the judge.

"Doctor Killian, you have been found guilty by a jury of your peers. I hereby sentence you to imprisonment for life at the territorial prison. Court is adjourned."

And thus did Doc begin his long journey to Yuma.

"Doc. Hey Doc!" boomed Big Bill's voice. "What's the matter with you tonight? Can't you keep your mind on one little card game? Come on. Ante up or do something. Don't just sit there and daydream."

Doc awoke from his dream of the past, examined his hand, and said: "I'll fold. No use trying to beat a crooked dealer like you."

"Aw now, Doc," grinned Big Bill. "You know I never bottom dealt in my whole life."

Maybe not, thought Doc. But maybe you once dealt me the worst hand of luck I ever had. He settled back to wait out the hand and watched the five men playing cards at his poker table.

And he wondered, *Which one am I going to have to kill?*

Chapter 4

It was hot in the kitchen of Doc's house. As Big Bill continued his dealing Doc remembered how hot it had been at
Yuma.

Yuma, Arizona Territory, was located a short piece down-
stream from where the Gila River joins the Colorado. Here the
Gila Trail, a route long used by the early pioneers, met the
river.

As a town site, it was a poor selection. Daytime temperatures
during the hot season were generally above 100 degrees. Many
days out of the year the thermometer stayed close to 120 degrees. Hot, dry, dusty, isolated, and primitive best described
Yuma.

After Doc's conviction he was hauled off to Yuma in a stagecoach. Maybe Amos couldn't face taking his old friend to
prison, or maybe he hated the sight of him. However that was,
he delegated the job to his deputy, Sid Harris.

For two days and one night the two men jolted and bounced
together on the rough ride along the Gila Trail with Doc
handcuffed to Sid's left hand. The coach in which they rode
carried the mail. Human passengers were just so much excess
baggage. Aside from periodic rest stops to change horses, there
was never more than thirty minutes rest in the thirty-six hour
journey to the prison at Yuma.

Doc and Sid didn't do much talking during the trip. Sid was
a naturally silent type of man. Doc didn't feel much like
talking.

After being shackled to the deputy for twelve hours, Doc's

wrist was getting sore. During one of the stops he showed his chafed wrist to the deputy. Sid pulled a key out of his pocket and unlocked the cuffs. "You wasn't aimin' to run off from me was you?" he asked.

"Where would I run to?" Doc replied. "You got the gun and the canteen. It's a long ways between water holes out here in the desert."

"I'm sorry about all this, Doc. You know I'm just doing my duty."

"Sure, I know." Doc rubbed the raw skin on his wrist. "I don't blame you, Sid. It's just the whole damned situation. Here you're hauling my ass off to Yuma for a crime I didn't commit, and all the time the real killer is sitting off in some cantina having himself a good laugh."

Sid glumly observed his prisoner. "If that's true, what you figure to do about it?"

"For one thing I'm going to see about getting out of the territorial prison just as soon as I can," Doc said earnestly. "Then I'm going to get back to Gila Crossing and start looking for that cantina. The first guy I catch laughing there had better have a good reason for being happy."

"Aw, for chrissakes, Doc. Ain't you got enough trouble already without thinking about going gunning for somebody? Hell. They'll just lock you up again and then I'll have to haul you off to Yuma again." Sid smiled ruefully. "I can't spend all my life running you down to prison."

Doc turned to climb back into the stagecoach. "I'll see if I can't get somebody else to take me back next time. But I sure aim to catch that son of a bitch that killed Jeanne."

"I wish you luck," said Sid as he regained his own seat and the coach drove on.

The stagecoach arrived at Yuma late in the afternoon. The sun was still high. The thermometer read 116 degrees. There was no shade. The deputy and his captive got out at the stage depot and walked the short distance to the prison. To Doc, it was the longest walk of his life.

The Arizona Territorial Prison sat on top of a hill surmount-

ing Yuma. On the north side of the hill was the Colorado
River. To the east was the Gila River. South and west were
town and desert. It was an ideal spot for a prison. The strong
current of the two rivers made escape in that direction almost
impossible. On the land side the desert stretched for endless
miles. Any escaped prisoner foolhardy enough to start across
the desert on foot would soon die from lack of water. Or else
the Indians would capture him.

There was a standing reward of fifty dollars for escaped prisoners. This was a fortune to the desert Indians. Any white man
they found afoot in the desert was soon returned to the prison
for the reward. The bounty notice stipulated that the prisoner
could be returned alive or dead. It didn't matter.

Most of the escaped prisoners were returned alive. It was a
matter of cold logistics. It was simpler to have the prisoner
walk back on his own feet than to have to carry a dead body.

Doc and Sid, still handcuffed together, walked up the road
that curved around the hill and came to the main gate, simply
large double doors in a wooden stockade. There was a smaller
door cut into one of the larger double doors. This door allowed
the guards and prisoners to pass in and out of the prison compound. There was a guardhouse outside the main gate.

Doc was among the first prisoners ever to be confined at
Yuma. The Arizona Territorial Prison had come into being
only that year. The cornerstone had been laid as recently as
April 28, 1876. The first group of prisoners, fifteen in number,
had helped construct the prison. By July 1, 1876, the prisoners
had completed their new permanent quarters. Before that they
had been housed in the jail maintained by the Yuma County
sheriff.

The new prison consisted of two stone cells and an adobe
building, which had two prison rooms, a kitchen, a dining hall,
a hall room for guards, a dispensary, and the superintendent's
quarters. There was a water reservoir, complete with pump,
boiler, and engine. Water was pumped up to the stone storage
tank from the muddy Colorado River. There was also a well-
equipped blacksmith shop.

When Doc arrived at the prison it was August 1876. He was prisoner number sixteen.

Sid presented his convict to the guard at the gatehouse. That guard directed him to take Doc over to the superintendent's quarters located inside the prison compound, directly across from the main gate. The door guard opened the small entryway in the main gate so Doc and Sid could pass through into the prison yard.

The door slammed shut behind them. Doc felt cold in spite of the heat. It was as though the place were squeezing in around him, crushing, trapping him. His world had suddenly shrunk to a couple of acres in size. He didn't like the looks of it.

There was an office located in one of the rooms of the superintendent's quarters. When Doc and Sid entered, the guard went out and soon returned with the superintendent, Mr. George M. Thurlow.

"Sir"—Sid stood with his hat in his one free hand—"I'm Deputy Sheriff Harris from Piñon County. Would you please sign this receipt of delivery for my prisoner?"

He didn't look at Doc. So that's how it was done—like signing for a bushel of potatoes or a side of beef.

The superintendent examined Sid's paper, signed it, and gave it back to him. The deputy then handed him a sheaf of papers that furnished a record of Doc's trial, conviction, and sentence. Sid then unlocked the handcuffs that bound him to Doc. Their eyes met for a moment. *I'll follow you one day*, Doc promised silently. *And when I do, the real killer will have a long bill to pay*. Doc was left with the superintendent and a guard.

"Killian"—Superintendent Thurlow had a commanding voice—"you're a convicted felon and have been given a life sentence in this prison. You can make the time that you spend here easy or hard. It all depends upon your attitude. There are rules and regulations which you must follow here. If you cooperate with the officers of this prison, you may in time earn certain privileges that will ease your confinement." He cleared his throat.

"If, on the other hand, you make trouble, you'll find your life here will be most difficult. The decision is yours. Guard, take this prisoner and process him."

"Yes sir," the guard nudged Doc. "All right, Killian, let's go."

The guard took Doc out of the office and into a supply room where Doc's civilian clothes were taken away from him and he was issued a prison uniform. *Get through it. Take whatever they hand out. Just stay alive. Alive so you can go back.* He was ordered to take a bath. Then his hair was clipped short. After the bath and haircut he was photographed in his prison uniform. His new suit had vertical black and gray stripes.

"Killian"—the guard's tone of voice was bored, droning— "you're allowed one hat, one extra shirt, an extra pair of trousers, two pairs of underwear, two pairs of socks, two handkerchiefs, two towels, and one pair of shoes. You are also allowed to have one toothpick, one toothbrush, and both a fine and a coarse comb. Photographs of friends and relatives are approved. You can have mail, passed through the prison office and censored. There's a regular ration of tobacco." The guard fished out a plug of chewing tobacco and handed it to Doc.

Doc handed the plug back to the guard. "Thanks, but I don't chew."

The guard grunted and thrust the tobacco back into Doc's hand. "Guess you ain't never been in prison before. If you don't use it yourself, keep it fer trading with the other cons.

"You can have books. You gotta write your name plainly in ink at three different places across the printed text. You get two sheets and two pillow cases for bedding. All bedding and clothing has to be marked with your prison number. During cold weather you'll be issued one blanket."

Doc picked up his supply rations and was taken to the cellblock, cells back to back, constructed of solid stone taken from a quarry located on top of prison hill.

The walls were three feet thick. There was a single iron-grid door on each end of the cellblock. A solid wall separated the two cells so there was no communication between the cells from the inside. There were no windows. The roof was of stone arch construction.

In size the cells measured about seven feet wide by eight feet long and fourteen feet high. There were two tiers of wooden bunks along the outside walls. These beds rose four high, giving sleeping space for eight men to the cell. In the hot climate of Yuma the bunks nearest the floor were the coolest. Doc, being the last arrival, got the remaining space on the top right-hand tier.

There were no lockers to store personal articles. No chairs. Sanitary facilities consisted of one slop bucket and another bucket for drinking water.

Doc was dismayed with his new living quarters. The wooden bunks were crude and had never been painted. The mattress covers were filthy and almost black from body grime. The stench from the uncovered slop bucket nearly gagged him. Even during his days of army service, out on the battlefields, he had lived better than this.

Resolutely he closed his mind to his physical surroundings. This was something he would have to endure! No inconvenience could obscure his purpose. Somehow he would survive the prison and get on with his search for the person responsible for his being at Yuma.

"Where do I store my extra gear?" asked Doc, looking around the cell.

"Under the mattress," came the laconic reply.

Doc climbed up the tier of bunks to his new resting place and raised the mattress. An army of bedbugs and cockroaches scurried around and tried to disappear into the cracks between the wooden bed boards. Not all of them made it into a crack. There were just too many bugs for the available space. Doc grimly placed his extra clothing under the mattress and climbed back down to floor level.

"Seems a mite crowded under that mattress," he told the guard.

"You'll get used to it. Come on. It's suppertime."

The guard led Doc to the mess hall, an adobe building next

to the kitchen. There were two long wooden tables down the center of the room with wooden benches on each side. The other fifteen convicts had just returned from their work assignment and were lined up at the kitchen serving window.

Doc went to the end of the line. The older cons looked at him with interest. They said nothing as they picked up their tin plates, loaded with food, and moved over to sit down at the table. When Doc got up to the head of the line he was given a tin pie plate, a metal cup, and a spoon. There were no knives or forks.

On his plate was piled the supper for Tuesday, beef stew and two pieces of bread. His cup was filled with coffee, unsweetened. Doc was to find out later that the menu never changed. There was one daily bill of fare for each day of the week. It varied from day to day, but aside from occasional extras on Sundays and holidays, the food was always the same.

Doc took his supper and sat down at one of the tables. The other seven men seated with him were busy wolfing down their food. No one took time to greet Doc. As a new man, he was at the bottom of the prison hierarchy. He ate his supper in silence.

When all the prisoners had finished eating, a guard gave the signal for them to return their eating equipment to the kitchen serving window. A guard, posted at the window, made sure each man turned in his plate, spoon, and cup. Then the sixteen prisoners were formed into two groups and marched off to their cells to be locked in for the night.

As each man entered the cell, he immediately laid himself down on his own bunk. There was no room in the cell to do otherwise. Doc climbed up to his lofty bed, the guard locked the steel door, and the convicts were left to their own devices for the rest of the night.

As soon as the guard left, Doc's cellmates started in.

"What's your name?" asked the man in the opposite top bunk.

"Killian," replied Doc.

"What you in for?" came up from below.

"Murder," said Doc.

His cellmates stared at Doc with new measures of respect. Here was a man who was bound to go straight to the top in prison society. There were two classes of prisoners at Yuma. Those who were lifers, and those who were short termers. The lifers were all in for murder. The short-time men had all committed lesser felonies. The lifers formed an elite caste. They were looked up to by the short termers.

Of the seven men who shared the same cell with Doc, four were Mexican, two were Indian and one was Caucasian. The other white man was a murderer by the name of William Mall. He was short and stocky, with a fierce-looking mustache and a bulbous red nose. He held the distinction of being the first prisoner held in the new institution.

The four Mexicans, whose names were Jesus, José, Angel, and Angelito, were in for robbery or assault. They resembled each other in every particular except size. They all had black hair, swarthy complexions, and a general slimness. However, their height varied in six-inch gradations down from the six feet two inch length of Jesus to the four feet eight inch shortness of Angelito.

The two Indians, Ho-Chit and Nas Good, had been convicted of grand larceny, a blanket indictment that usually meant cattle rustling. Ho-Chit was short and grossly fat. Nas Good stood above medium height and had an unnatural thinness about him.

Doc surveyed his bunk mates. The common denominator of close-cropped hair and striped prison garb had robbed them of their individuality. Aside from racial characteristics they could have all been brothers. And so they were. Brothers of the bug-infested, hot, sweltering, ovenlike stone cell. Doc rolled over on his back and studied the ceiling a scant two feet over his head.

Heat radiated downwards from the sun-heated stone roof of the cell. It beat upon Doc's body in pulsating waves. It was unbearably hot on the upper bunk. Soon Doc could stand the heat no longer.

He slipped over the side of his bunk and made his way to the floor of the cell. He could see that all of his cellmates were stark naked. They lay upon their grimy beds absorbing the punishing heat of Arizona desert summer; if not in comfort, at least in practiced resignation. Doc stripped off his clothes and returned to his bed.

"Welcome to the club," Mall saluted him with a grin, "reveille's at 5:45 A.M. Better get some sleep."

Doc tried to find a comfortable position. This was impossible. As soon as he lay still, bedbugs and cockroaches assaulted him. When he fought them off, he got even hotter. He didn't get any sleep that first night.

Early the next morning the prisoners were routed out of their cells. This being Wednesday, the breakfast menu consisted of beef steak, potatoes, bread, and coffee. Then the convicts were marched out to the stone quarry to begin a day of labor.

Since the new prison was fenced in with a wooden stockade, the first priority of building was to construct a permanent wall. This wall was to be made of adobe bricks erected on a foundation of granite stone.

The prisoners were split into two work parties. Those with the most seniority were given the easier task of making adobe bricks. The most recent additions to the prison population were set to work hacking out blocks of stone for the foundation. Doc was assigned to the quarry crew.

The stone quarry was located on the high point of prison hill where a natural outcropping of granite supplied stone for the wall foundations. It was hard, hot, dirty work, which went on all day except for a short break at noon for dinner.

The Arizona sun heated the granite outcropping until it seemed that the iron tools and the very rock itself would burn the hide off his hands. Doc's muscles weren't equal to the task at first. The sheer dead weight of handling the stone made his arms feel as if they were going to drop off. But the worst thing about the work was that he felt like a slave. One of Pharaoh's captives hewing out blocks for the pyramids. He applied himself to the task and drove himself harder than the sternest taskmaster of ancient Egypt. He was going to be a hard-working model prisoner if it killed him.

The prisoners worked in two-man teams. One man wielded a sledgehammer while his partner held a rock drill. When sufficient holes were drilled, they were filled with black powder, and the resulting explosion broke the solid rock into more manageable pieces. These pieces were roughly dressed with rock hammers and chisels and then stacked in a pile from which they would later be taken to fill the wall foundation trenches.

Day after day the quarry crew worked at making little rocks out of big rocks. They were guarded by two heavily armed men who carried both rifles and pistols. The standard guard rifle at the prison was the .44-40 Winchester lever-action repeating rifle. The pistols varied, as did the personalities of the guards, who were alike in one thing; they were all dead shots. No prisoners ever attempted escape during Doc's term at the prison.

For the first two weeks of his captivity Doc was given the task of holding the rock drill. His working partner, Bill Mall, handled the sledgehammer.

Because of his seniority Mall should have been working with the adobe crew, but some minor infraction of prison rules had brought the punishment of working on the quarry crew. He and Doc made a good team.

Doc never thought of escape. If he'd known the identity of Jeanne's killer, he'd probably have made some wild try for freedom, seeking enough time to go back and square accounts, no matter what happened to him afterwards. But he didn't know who the killer was. Vague suspicions rose in his mind. He remembered how Opal Johnson had told him that his five friends were all out of the room at the time Jeanne was killed. When he thought back on the situation it seemed like more than a coincidence. It didn't stand to reason that five men would leave a party at the same time. Maybe one of them had killed Jeanne. He'd have to think some more about that possibility.

He needed time. His only hope was a pardon, and to get that he'd have to be a model prisoner. Endure the heat and shame and grueling labor, but keep hold of the core of himself, of the driving purpose that was the only reason he wanted to live.

Somehow, someday, he'd leave this prison and then the man who'd sent him here and killed Jeanne was going to pay. Doc was ready to spend the rest of his life in jail. Just so the guilty man didn't escape.

"Hold 'er steady there, Killian." Mall swung his sledge. "I sure would hate to take a swing, miss the drill, and brain you. If I did that, they probably wouldn't ever let me go back to making bricks."

Doc grimaced. "I'll hold steady. Just see if you can concentrate on tapping that drill instead of me."

Together they drilled holes in the solid rock through the long days. Doc's hands blistered. The blisters broke. His hands caused him untold agony until calluses formed to relieve his suffering. By the end of two weeks, Doc's hands had healed and he had advanced from drill holder to sledge driver. At least he was the sledge driver part of the time. The two partners alternated their jobs mornings and afternoons.

The alternate drilling and blasting steadily ate away the crest of the stone hill. When sufficient rock had been broken loose, the entire work party was set to work dressing the stones.

When the stones had been all dressed, they were manhandled over to the storage pile. The stones were moved on rough wooden stretchers carried by two men.

Late one hot afternoon while the prisoners were stacking fresh dressed stone blocks on the storage pile, one of the blocks slipped loose from its handlers and struck a guard standing beside the storage pile. His scream brought work to a standstill. The rest of the quarry crew and the other guard came running up to the fallen man.

The remaining guard aimed his rifle at the convicts and ordered them to line up and face the stockade wall. Then he stooped and dragged the fallen rock off the injured man. The rock had hit the guard on his left upper arm, breaking the skin and causing a considerable amount of bleeding. Groaning as his comrade shifted the rock, the injured guard passed out from the pain of what was obviously a broken arm.

"Any of you men know how to set a broken arm?" the remaining guard threw at the prisoners.

No one moved or said anything. In prison you learn not to volunteer any information. And to help a guard—that wouldn't make for popularity.

"God dammit! I asked you bastards a question and I want an answer."

Doc said, "I can do it."

"O.K., get your ass over here and be quick about it. The rest of you keep on facing that wall or I'll blow your heads off."

Quickly Doc found a couple of short sticks to make a splint. He took off his shirt and ripped it for bandages.

"I'll need some help," he appealed to the guard.

"Mall," called the guard, "get over here on the double and lend a hand."

Under Doc's direction, Mall pulled on the arm until it straightened while the revived man moaned and swore. Doc applied the splints and bandages.

"I'm done," Doc said.

"You and Mall get a stone stretcher and load Jack on it," ordered the guard.

When the injured man was loaded, the guard had the rest of the quarry crew fall in behind Doc and Mall. Then they all marched out of the quarry and up to the main gate. The guard was carried off to his quarters, and the work crew were returned to their cells while the superintendent was informed as to what had happened.

Soon a guard called Doc out and marched him to the superintendent's office.

"Killian"—the super motioned for him to sit down—"where did you learn to set a broken arm?"

Doc was surprised by the question. "Why, I'm a doctor, sir. I thought you knew."

Thurlow reared back in his chair and digested this bit of information. "No. It's not mentioned in your admission papers.

Had I known, you would have been assigned a different work task than quarrying stone."

The super was a quick judge of men. His long experience as a lawman had given him the ability to sift out the competent. He made a quick decision.

"Killian, there's only one doctor in Yuma. He's quite often called away when we need him here. We have no regular prison physician. Would you care for the job?"

Hope stirred in Doc's breast. What better way to earn a pardon than to practice a traditionally respected profession? Besides, there were certainly some things he might be able to improve in the administration of the prison. He didn't even have to consider the question.

"I would be delighted to serve, sir."

Chapter 5

Doc had set some sort of a prison record. He moved from manual laborer to trustee in only two weeks. Trustees had certain privileges that were denied the common prisoner. However, Doc had to spend one more night in the common cell where he was returned after his interview.

"You done a right good piece of work on Jack's arm," the guard said admiringly. "Ol' Jack'll want to thank you when he gets back on duty."

"All in a day's work," Doc said.

"Maybe for you," the guard admitted, "but if you hadn't been on the spot, Jack would have had to wait a long time for the town sawbones to get out here and set that arm. Might a got blood poison. Jack won't forget."

Doc's bunk mates already knew about his promotion to trustee. The prisoner telegraph system had very quickly carried the news.

"Hey, Killian," Mall shouted at him, "why didn't you tell me you were a doctor?"

"You never asked me."

"How soon they gonna let you sleep out?" was Mall's next question.

Doc didn't know what he was talking about. "What do you mean about sleeping out?"

"Don't you know? When you get to be a trustee, they let you sleep someplace besides the cellblock."

Doc was still puzzled. "How did you know I was going to be a trustee?"

"The world is only so big here and the word gets around fast." Mall pulled on his mustache.

Doc and Mall settled back on their opposite bunks. "While you was talking to the super"—Mall rolled over on his side—"one of the other trustees kinda overheard the conversation. He told one of the assistant cooks. The assistant cook told the food server. The food server passed the word while the men were picking up their supper plates. Every con and guard in the place knows you're a doctor and that you're going to be a trustee. Congratulations. You're the fair-haired boy around here now."

Doc acknowledged the compliment by making a face. "The super asked me to be the prison doctor. I told him I'd take the job."

Mall whistled. "Christ, but you're lucky. That means you'll have the dispensary room all to yourself to sleep in. They'll probably move you over there tomorrow." He looked a little crestfallen. "Guess I'll have to get me a new working partner on the rock pile."

Doc grinned at his teammate. "Can't say I'll miss the rock pile. How long will it be before they move you back to the adobe crew?"

Mall crossed his fingers in the good luck sign. "Not long. I've about made up the credits I lost when I got in that fight with Ochoa."

"What was the fight about?"

"Nothing much." Mall had a mischievous look in his eyes. "We'd been mixing mud for the bricks and throwing it in the molds. I got a little careless and splashed some of my mud on Ochoa. He said that if I had as much cock in my pants as I had in my eye, I'd be quite a man. That's when I slugged him."

Doc and the rest of the men in the cell laughed. Mall made mock bowing motions from the cramped position of his bunk. "Now that you're going to be the resident physician of this establishment I guess we better start calling you Doc."

Doc was startled to hear how good that sounded. It had been a while since he'd been called by his nickname. For the first

time he wondered if there might not be something left to live
for besides his revenge. But one thing at a time. . . .

"Everyone used to call me that before I came to Yuma.
Here's the first place I've been called Killian for years."

"Doctor," came Angelito's soft voice from a lower bunk,
"could you see if you can get the cooks to put more chili in the
food. My stomach yearns for a little fire."

"I'll sure try, Angelito," Doc solemnly reassured him.

Jesus spoke next in his lilting Spanish-flavored English.
"Could something perhaps be done about the little bugs, Doctor? *La cucaracha* I do not mind so much. But the little bugs
they rob me of my sleep."

Doc always liked to hear Jesus talk. "I'll take it up with the
super."

"There is something comes to my mind." Angel frowned at
the effort. "*La agua* from the river is still plenty *colorado* when
I drink from the bucket. Could not something be done to make
my drink more—how you say—fluid?"

"I'm sure there must be some way to get more of the mud
out of the drinking water," agreed Doc. "If anybody asks me,
I'll give them some of my ideas."

José was concerned about odors. "The slop bucket"—he
pointed to the uncovered receptacle in the corner of the cell
next to his bunk—"smells bad. Sometimes at night it makes my
head to ache. When you see your friend the super, could this
not be mentioned?"

"He's not really my friend," Doc had to remind them. "Next
time I see him, though, I'll not only mention the slops, but I
think I can find a way to do away with the smell."

"It would be an act of kindness." José smiled his thanks.

Ho-Chit, the Apache Indian, who seldom spoke, pointed a
long finger at the chest of the other Indian, Nas Good.
"Cough," he said.

Doc had noticed Nas Good's cough. He had identified it as
being a symptom of incipient consumption. Most captive Indians got it sooner or later.

Doc nodded his head. "I'll do something for him if I can."

"Well, boys," Mall yawned largely, "it's time to break up this tea party and get some sleep. I don't know about the rest of you galoots, but I gotta go back to bustin' rock again tomorrow. Good night, Doc."

Doc lay back on his bunk savoring the sound of the old familiar name. He felt that he was no longer just a member of the prison records. He'd regained some measure of identity. He rolled over and went to sleep almost peacefully.

Next morning after breakfast the other cons were marched back to their work outside the stockade while a guard named Juan took Doc over to the dispensary room.

It was just a room located in the large adobe building. There was a bed in one corner. An examination table occupied the center. Along one wall were shelves that held various pharmaceuticals. There were also medical supplies and a kit of surgical tools.

"Here's where you work and sleep from now on," Juan waved spaciously around the room. "You must have made a big hit with the super. He said you didn't have to go back on the work party. As a trustee you can come and go as you please, so long as you stay in the prison yard. Mr. Thurlow said to check over the supplies in here and decide if you need anything else. When you get finished with that he wants to talk to you."

Juan sat down while Doc stowed his extra clothing under the mattress on the bed. He was relieved to see that the bug population had not followed him to his new room. A quick-eyed inventory showed there were enough common drugs and supplies on the shelves to serve the needs of the prison population. Whoever had set up the dispensary had known his job.

"Seems like there's enough of everything here. I might as well go talk to Mr. Thurlow now." Doc straightened his uniform.

Juan walked Doc back over to the superintendent's office. As he left him there he said, "See ya around, Doc."

Doc's heart lifted even more. Even the guards had evidently decided to accept him as a doctor instead of a con. He went into the office and found the prison administrator working at his desk.

Doc snapped to attention. "You sent for me, sir?"

Thurlow turned from his papers. "Yes, Killian, I did. Sit down."

Doc sat down in a chair facing his keeper. George Thurlow had a full black-gray streaked beard and mustache. He had kind eyes and bore himself with grace.

"Why are you in here, Killian?"

"For murder, sir."

Thurlow shook his head. "I didn't mean the formal charge. I meant why would an educated man, a physician, one who had dedicated his life to saving other lives, commit murder?"

"I didn't do it, sir." Doc gazed at him levelly.

The superintendent looked straight into Doc's blue eyes.

"I'm not going to try and second guess the judge and jury that sent you here. It wouldn't be the first time a mistake in justice has been made. What concerns me is how you're going to serve your time."

"Day by day, sir. Just like any other convict." *Except I want out more than most.*

Thurlow nodded his head in approval. "I have ordered you relieved from the work parties. As the prison doctor and a trustee you're going to have a lot of time on your hands. What do you propose to keep yourself busy?"

Doc smiled as he remembered the conversation with his cellmates. "For a start, sir, I'd like to see if I can't solve the bug problem in the cellblock."

"More power to you, Killian, if you can. What else?"

"Sanitation and water supply could be improved. I have a few ideas."

The superintendent nodded. "I'm in favor of that. Let me know what you need and I'll see you get it."

"Thank you, sir. Another thing. One of the Indians is coming down with consumption. Would it be possible to have some sort of isolation cell for him to be kept separate from the other men?"

Thurlow did some mental calculations. "Probably. We'll work something out." He turned back to his cluttered desk. "You better get started on the bugs. I've got a lot of paperwork to do here. Tell Juan what supplies you need. He can get you a small work detail to help with the job."

Doc stood up. "Thank you, sir. I'll do what I can." He left the office and walked over to the main gate where he called for Juan.

"What you want, Doc?"

"I need lye and hot water. Also stone crocks to mix it in and a couple of men. Could you get Jesus and Angelito off the work gang to help me?"

"Sure thing." Juan nodded. "I'll be right back. Don't go away."

Doc waited. Soon the guard came back with the two helpers. Jesus and Angelito were mystified as to why they had been taken off the work detail in the middle of the day.

"I'm going to send you boys to war." Doc gave them a military salute.

"Oh, no, señor doctor." Jesus protested. "I'm a robber, not a soldier. I could never kill anyone."

"Nor am I a soldier," affirmed Angelito. "You must remember that I am a lover, not a fighter."

Doc smiled at the two men. "This is a war in which you'll be proud to be soldiers. You'll be glad to fight the good fight. To kill without mercy. I am going to make bug-killing soldiers out of you."

"Es verdad." Jesus bowed. "In that kind of war I shall be a soldier, even a colonel."

Angelito blew a kiss with his hand. "I shall love my work."

Doc and his army went to work. They pulled all the mattresses off the bunks and spread them in the sunshine of the prison yard. Then, having mixed a strong lye solution, they scrubbed the bare bunks and walls and floors. Bugs by the thousands died from the lye solution.

Doc and his crew beat the mattresses with sticks to dislodge as many bugs as possible. They turned the mattresses repeatedly and let the hot Arizona sun bake and purify them. By nightfall the prisoners could all sleep without suffering from insect bites.

And so it went. Doc put lime in the slop buckets and provided lids to confine the odors. He prevailed upon the prison authorities to build a second water tank so the mud from the river water had a chance to settle out in one tank while the men drank from the other.

Under his direction an infirmary cell was constructed on top of the cellblock so that prisoners suffering from consumption and other contagious diseases could be isolated. Nas Good was the first patient to enter the new infirmary cell.

Doc ran the infirmary and instituted a morning sick call. He treated the sick prisoners with common sense and the medicines he had on hand. He performed minor surgery when needed and patched up cuts and abrasions suffered by the men working on the stone quarry crew. He kept busy. But still, during the three long years, there was much time to think.

He thought mostly of Jeanne—and the revenge he would have for her death.

He was tortured by loneliness; her memory ate away at his vitals until at times he thought of suicide. What could life ever be without her? Her warmth, laughter, kisses? It would be easy to end his own suffering. A fatal injection of some drug from his medical supply would do the trick. But the need to punish her murderer kept him from doing away with himself.

He also thought a great deal about his five friends. Of how they had all testified against him at his trial. The change that had come over their relationships after they had apparently made up their minds he was the killer. If they could suspect him, why couldn't he suspect them? What was Noel trying to cover up when he gave such positive testimony about his guilt? Why did Amos keep insisting he was the only man that could be placed at the scene of the crime? Where were they when Jeanne died?

Doc brooded so much over Jeanne and the actions of his former friends that at times he thought he was losing his mind.

3

The only thing that saved his sanity was the determination to be free again someday.

That, and the fact that he played poker in his spare time. Gambling was forbidden in the prison, but Doc played for matches with the other trustees and even some of the guards. It helped time to pass during his years of confinement.

After Doc had been locked up for two and one-half years, he had pretty well settled into a daily routine. Up at reveille for breakfast. Sick call after the morning meal. Supervise the sanitation crew before noon. Dinner. Report to the superintendent or his assistant. Make rounds in the infirmary. Supper. Poker until bedtime. It was a simple life. A dull life. Like all other convicts the world over, Doc did his time, day by day.

Then there came an epidemic of cholera. Everyone in the prison, cons and guards alike, came down with the disease. Contaminated water from one of the water tanks was the culprit. According to their physical condition the victims suffered a light or heavy case of cholera. Soon the prison was one large pesthouse.

Doc, because he never drank water except as coffee or tea, was not affected by the disease. He worked tirelessly day and night during the epidemic to save his patients with help from the town doctor and some civilian volunteers. By the time the disease had run its course, Doc had saved all but three convicts and one guard.

By that time Doc was exhausted and trembling, near collapse. He staggered to his quarters and slept clear around the clock.

When he woke up, he had become a minor celebrity in the prison and town of Yuma. He was treated with a new degree of respect by all of his expatients. The guards brought him special food and tobacco—and even a little contraband whiskey.

The prisoners presented him with handcrafted tokens of their respect. One man made him an inlaid wooden box for his small personal items. Another collected enough horse tail hair to weave him a bridle. Doc got so many presents, his sleeping room resembled a bazaar. He traded most of his presents to the guards for special food, which he gave back to the prisoners. Doc and the men on prison hill formed a mutual admiration society.

One day the superintendent sent for Doc.

Doc entered the prison office. "You sent for me, sir?"

"Yes, I did. Sit down, Doctor Killian."

Doc sat down, amazed that the super should give him this honorary form of address. In all the time he had been at Yuma, even though the guards and prisoners all called him "Doc," this was the first time the head prison officer had called him by anything but his surname.

"Doctor," said the warden, "on behalf of the entire population of this prison I want to convey our thanks for what you did during the epidemic. You served far and above the call of duty. Without your help many more of us would not be alive today."

"Thank you, sir." Doc colored though the praise was sweet. "I was only doing my duty."

Thurlow brushed that aside. "You've been a great influence for good at this institution. You've improved our sanitation system and water supply. Before you came our sick and wounded sometimes suffered because we didn't have a resident doctor. All things considered, I feel that you have more than repaid your debt to society. I am going to recommend to the governor of this territory that he issue you a pardon."

Doc was dumbfounded. He had not expected this. It was a gift from the blue. Five years at least he'd expected, probably ten, maybe fifteen or twenty. But to go free now—"Thank you, sir," he managed to say. "Would you have any idea as to when I might be released?"

"It's April." Thurlow consulted his wall calendar. "I should think by the end of July you'll be able to walk out of here."

"I can't thank you enough!" Doc rose to his feet.

The super stood and held out his hand. "Thank you, Doctor."

Doc moved out of the superintendent's office in a kind of daze. At last it was all falling into place. He was going to be turned loose.

But where to start in finding Jeanne's killer? Obviously his former five friends would bear some checking out. Each one of the men was going to have to account for his whereabouts when Jeanne was killed. Why had Big Bill insisted on telling the jury that he thought Doc had accidentally killed his wife? Did Bill know more than he had let on? And what about Bryce's story? It had seemed a little too glib in the courtroom. Bryce had a reputation as a lady-killer. Maybe he really was one. Even Jim Balinte had gone out of his way to wash his hands of the case. Why? Did he want all suspicion pointed away from himself?

The next three months dragged by as though they would never pass. Each day Doc and his well-wishers played the game of asking if word from the governor had been received. It wasn't until the middle of June that word filtered down from the territorial capital that the governor was definitely considering the pardon.

A petition recommending the pardon was made up and signed by all the guards and prisoners. This, along with a second petition signed by many of the residents of Yuma, was forwarded to the governor. Almost another month went by with no word from the capital. Then, one day towards the end of July, the pardon came.

It was a full pardon. Doc's rights as a citizen were restored. His sentence was commuted. He was a free man again.

Doc turned in his prison uniform and put on the same clothes he had worn when committed. The prison officials offered to provide him with a new suit at state expense. Knowing the quality of such clothing, Doc preferred to wear his own. He was given a ticket back to Gila Crossing. After making his good-byes he left the prison forever and returned to freedom.

And his purpose.

"Doc! Hey Doc!" came Big Bill's foghorn voice cutting into his memories. "Do I gotta wake you up for every deal tonight? Act alive, will you. Is it all right with you if I pass the deal on to the sheriff here? Or do you want to make up some new rules?"

Doc looked from Bill to Amos. "Oh, I guess we may as well play by the rules. Go ahead and give him the cards. I don't think he can do a worse job of dealing than you've been doing."

"Thanks a lot," Bill growled as he passed the deck to the sheriff.

Doc watched Amos out of the corner of his eyes. *Is this the man who sent me to Yuma for three years? Amos has always been handy with a gun. Now let's see how handy he is with the cards.*

Chapter 6

Amos, with the ease and skill of the fast-draw artist, dealt cards like greased lightning. His practiced hands spun out cards around the circle of the table in a rhythmic cadence of moving beauty. If such commonplace objects as cards could be described as being graceful, then Amos' dealing made them that way. It was a pleasure to watch him deal.

Bob Noel lit up a long, black, ten-cent cigar. "Hoo boy, you threw me the right ones that time. I'll stand pat."

"Hit me again." Jim Balinte's kind eyes twinkled.

Bryce crossed his eyes, let his mouth go slack, and made his voice sound like the village idiot. "Two of your best, maestro."

Doc had a hard time keeping his face straight after looking at Bryce. "One ought to do me, Amos."

"Lo and behold, he done worked him a miracle," sang Bill. "The man gave me five cards that match for a change. No more for me."

In one fluid movement, Amos picked up his hand, quickly threw down two cards, and then drew two new ones. All present studied their final hands for a moment.

Noel blew a cloud of cigar smoke towards the ceiling. "Gentlemen, in all my years of banking experience I have never seen a more certain proposition than that which meets my eyes at the moment. I propose to open the bidding with a slight token of my newly minted faith. I think I'll bet twenty dollars—gold." He spun out a gold piece on the table.

Jim Balinte gulped, gravely considered the pasteboards he held in his hands and gave a philosophical shrug. "Men often live and die by their wits. Surely a man can do no less in a friendly game of cards. I, sir, shall see you." He placed a twenty-dollar greenback in the pot.

"I don't suppose it's really possible to have five aces." Bryce pulled a lock of his long hair down over his eyes and pretended to have trouble reading his cards. "However, I can assure the assembled company that I do have five equally valuable cards. Therefore, I'll match the picayune advancement of fortune made by our esteemed financial advisor and stay with you."

What had gotten into the players that they had so suddenly jumped from one dollar bets to twenty? Was this a test of some sort? Did they want to see if Doc had lost his nerve in prison? Well, be damned to them! He could still play poker with the best.

"Twenty dollars is a little measley for my tastes, boys," he said. "But if that's all you want to play for, count me in."

Bill reached a massive hand into his hip pocket and brought out a fistful of money. "I shoed a whole big bunch of wild horses this past week and everybody paid in cash. I think I'll just lend a bit of my ill-gotten gains to the pot." He peeled off two tens.

"I sure don't know what you cheapskates are betting on." Amos gave a lopsided smile. "I could have sworn I knew every card I double-dealt to everyone. Must be losing my touch as a dealer. I'll stay." He added to the pot.

Bob Noel riffled his çards. Clasping them tightly together in his hand, he assumed an air of gravity. "It's always been my experience that when the going gets tough, the tough get going. You fellow travelers have to meet my collateral before you see my cards. I'm raising thirty more dollars—gold."

Something funny was happening in this game. Even banker Bob couldn't afford these kind of stakes. Surely the joke would run its course and the other players would drop out. But no, the betting continued.

"Just as you say, sir. The race is not always to the swiftest, but quite often falls to the onslaught of he who gets there the firstest with the mostest. I'm calling you." Jim added his raise to the pile.

Bryce grandly threw out a ten and a twenty. "Obviously you pikers think you're playing with a piker. Here are my thirty further iron men and I wish I could say as much for the present company."

Did Doc's fellow players think he was broke and couldn't match their bets? He might have spent three years in prison, but that didn't automatically make him a pauper. His medical practice had been lucrative and he still had plenty of cash waiting for him when he came home. "No problem, fellows. Count me in on your little raise."

"I'm sure as hell going to have to shoe me some more horses, but I'll stay." Bill extracted thirty dollars from his handful and placed it on the table.

Amos just nodded his head and threw thirty dollars in the pot.

"Very well, gentlemen of the board," sighed Bob, "I want you all to see just what a lollapoloosa looks like. And please note that only one of these is allowed in any one evening of card playing." He laid down five cards that did not match nor add up to any conceivable poker hand.

Jim had one pair.

Bryce had two low pairs.

Bill fanned out three of a kind.

Doc held a royal flush.

The blood rushed to Doc's head. His anger rose like floodwater breaking through a dam. So that was it! They really were trying to make him a gift of money. Amos must have marked the deck. They thought they could make up with money what he had suffered at their hands over the three years in prison. It was time to call their bluff. He would be double damned if he was going to put up with their charity!

"All right you double-dealing sons of bitches!" Doc jumped up from his chair. "I'll see you all in hell before I touch any of that pot. I don't need your damned money."

The other card players sat in their chairs like wooden Indians. No sound existed in the room except for sharp intakes of breath. It was as though Doc had slapped them in their collective faces. And, of course, he had.

Doc glared at his dumbstruck friends. Anger prodded him on. *Careful. Mustn't say too much.* But being mad was natural, and he might as well give them something to chew on. "I've had a lot of time to think about you birds. Where the hell were you when I needed you?"

The five men stirred uneasily in their chairs. They cast covert glances at one another as Doc blazed on. "Not a one of you offered much support when I needed it most. Only one person in this whole town had the decency to come and see me while I was in jail awaiting trial, a woman I hardly know. Opal Johnson at least tried to show me I was still a human being. Did any of you give a damn about how I felt?" Doc glanced from one man to the next, men who had been his best friends, who'd let him down—and one—which one?—might be a murderer.

"Oh, what's the use of talking to you?" Doc knew he had to cut it off before he gave away his determination, warned the man he had to uncover. He pushed his chair away from the table and turned to walk away.

"Just a minute, Doc." Jim, gentle Jim Balinte, looked at Doc with compassionate eyes, spread his hands in helpless bewilderment. "No one understands better than us what you have been through. By the same token, can you understand what we've been through? We, who once were and still consider ourselves to be your friends. We have had to live for the past three years with the realization that we failed you in your hour of need."

Doc resumed his seat. His eyes searched Jim's face and saw truth. He kept still as Jim continued.

"It wasn't easy for us to turn our backs on you, Doc." Jim lowered his eyes. "At the time Jeanne died, all reason left us in our grief for what had happened. We thought then, and we still do, that you killed her."

Doc started to protest. Jim reached over and gently touched his shoulder. "With the passing of time, we've accepted that something drove you to kill the person you loved best. It's hap-

pened a thousand times before. All married men long to kill
their wives at one time or another. And most do in numerous
small and petty ways of daily living. Some do it with words and
spite. Others with unconcern for their needs as women. Only
the bravest men do it with a gun."

Doc just stared at him. Jim took a deep breath and plunged
on. "There's such a thin, red line between love and hate; it's a
mystery more marriages don't end in death. No man knows
what demons drive some other man across the line. Each man
must conquer or yield to his own urgings."

There was no movement in the room. The other poker
players seemed to have shifted into the background. It were as
though only Doc and Jim were present.

Jim's voice shook. "Doc, on behalf of all of us here, I ask you
to forgive us. We too have suffered with you. Let what is past
be forgotten. Can't we regain a measure of our old friendship?
Isn't it possible for us to pick up the pieces of our existence and
once again, if not love, at least have compassion for one another?"

Doc sat still and considered Jim's words. Friendship? Compassion? How could he feel either till he'd avenged Jeanne, his
own years in prison? The past still owned him, the woman he'd
lost, the mystery of why she'd been killed, the outrage and bitter hurt at being let down by his friends, the community he'd
served.

Forgive? Not till the real murderer was dead! And that killer
could possibly be one of these five men.

"Jim speaks for all of us." Bill's voice rumbled from the
depths of his wide throat.

"You've paid your debt to the law, Doc," pleaded Amos.
"Now let us pay ours to you."

Bob stared fixedly at the table.

"We've been damned fools!" Bryce was serious for a change.
"Don't you be one, too, Doc."

Doc had to say something. Only one of these men might be
the one he sought. Was it fair to be so unbending, so unforgiv-
ing, to the other four? It was hard to utter the words, but

finally he did. "I'm sorry. I've had this sticking in my craw for so long that I had to spit it out. I think I've got a right to be bitter about what's happened." Doc looked each of his friends in the eye as his glance swept around the table.

The other men returned Doc's scrutiny. Slowly all of them stood up. Doc faced them. Better speak reasonable words that would lull the killer, make him think Doc had no plans for vengeance. "Give me time to get this poison out of my system and then maybe we can all go back to being friends again."

"That's good enough for me." Jim gave Doc a warm, strong embrace.

Amos stepped around the table and punched Doc lightly on his upper arm. "I knew you'd come to your senses."

Bill gave Doc a bear hug that took him by surprise and almost broke one of his ribs.

Bryce stuck out his hand. "You got a deal, Doc. Shake on it?"

Doc grasped the hand and shook it. *Which man? Which friend?*

Bob took out his pocket watch and consulted the time. "Gentlemen, it's time we took ourselves to our respective domiciles. We don't want to overstay our welcome."

The five men wished Doc good night, recovered the money they'd thrown in the pot, and left.

Doc sank back down at the poker table and considered the possibilities. There was no tangible point from which to start his search for the murderer. True, he thought he had five suspects, but how to pinpoint the right one?

From what two of the men had said at the trial, Doc knew where they'd claimed to be at the time of the killing.

Amos had testified that he was on the front porch talking to his deputy, Sid Harris. Doc would look Sid up and verify that story.

Jim, in his testimony, had said he was in the kitchen getting some spice for his drink. It should be easy enough to talk with Noel's cook, Delia O'Connor. She would still be working at the Noel house since she was a longtime fixture in that establishment. Doc made a mental note to go to see Delia at his earliest chance.

Where had the other three men been? At a big house party like they had all attended on the night of the murder, people were always coming and going. It would take questioning and snooping around to locate the whereabouts of the other three men, but it would be possible.

Lots of people in Gila Crossing would remember the night of the party. Doc would track down his quarry cautiously, beginning with learning for certain the location of every man at the critical moment.

But what if he was on the wrong track? Could someone else have done the killing? Mentally he went over all the evidence, as he had so many times during the years at Yuma. There was the possibility that some unknown person had entered the library through the outside door, killed Jeanne, and then vanished without a trace. He would have to check out everything. Try to find a witness who had seen a stranger leaving the Noel house on the night of the murder.

He felt as he did when he used to go into the Superstition Mountains above Gila Crossing to hunt mountain lions. It was always hazardous to climb up into the trackless peaks and seek the elusive cat. Dangerous because you never knew at what moment on the trail you might suddenly come upon a wounded or cornered lion that was ready to turn and hunt the hunter. In Doc's time he had been one of the best lion hunters in Piñon County. He hoped he hadn't forgotten his hunting skills.

It was late. Doc blew out the kerosene lamps and went to bed.

Tomorrow he would start his hunt.

Chapter 7

The next morning Doc got up early, made his breakfast, shaved, dressed carefully, and started his walk around Gila Crossing.

Gila Crossing was the county seat of Piñon County. It sat more or less on the banks of the Gila River, depending where the banks were that particular year. Like most western rivers, the Gila changed its course from year to year. Most of the year it was a turbid, meandering stream that flowed quietly past the town site. During times of high water, it changed into a raging torrent, twisting and gouging out new channels at random.

An ancient Indian culture had grown up along the Gila long before the first white man came. These Indians, the Hohokam, had a system of irrigation canals that watered extensive fields of corn and beans. The Hohokams survived for a long period and had enough leisure to build rather complex cities of adobe.

The desert soil of Arizona, when dug out and mixed with straw and water, hardened in the dry air and became like cement. Great two- and three-story apartment houses were built in the cities. Long, ramparted walls surrounded each village. Extensive trade was carried on throughout the length of the Gila Valley between the Indian communities. Trade routes ran west across the desert to the Pacific Ocean. It was a unique and extensive culture. Then it all ended.

Perhaps the water table of the desert land rose from the continued irrigation and drowned out the agricultural system, or the mineral salts from the river water built up till it poisoned the crops. From whatever cause, the civilization of the Hohokam had long vanished except for a few scattered ruins.

One of the most impressive of these Indian remains was the Casa Grande about 10 miles southwest of Gila Crossing. It was still an imposing structure. In its time it had been a three-story complex of rooms and probably served as a watchtower. The first white man to visit the Casa Grande was Father Font, a Spanish Jesuit priest, who said Mass in one of its rooms on Christmas Day, 1775.

The Casa Grande was a favorite picnic site for the people of Gila Crossing; it was a pleasant ride out from town. Many a Sunday afternoon outing was made to this place. Doc and his friends had often visited there.

The town of Gila Crossing, a typical western frontier town of the late 1800s, was dominated by the courthouse. Surrounding the courthouse were the houses in which the townspeople lived. Some of the houses were brick, some were wooden, but the majority of them were adobe—thick, solid, desert cement houses that withstood the baking heat of the hot months and the driving cold winds of winter.

The business section of Gila Crossing was one main street along which were situated the hotel, newspaper office, saloon, cafe, bank, general store, undertaking establishment, and livery stable. The sheriff's office was located in the front of the jail at the end of the main street.

Gila Crossing wasn't very big, not nearly as large as Phoenix or Tucson, but it was the largest town in Piñon County.

Doc left his house, walked over to the main street, and started down the boardwalk. In front of the Gila Crossing Hotel several loafers were whittling and spitting as they passed the time of day.

"Howdy, Doc." One of the men quit whittling long enough to smile a greeting. "Glad to see you back. How were things over to Yuma?"

Doc shrugged. "I can't recommend it as a health resort."

The idlers laughed. And relaxed. Doc could almost guess their thoughts. *Good old Doc—he's not going to be a sorehead. Hey, why do you reckon he killed his wife?*

Another of the whittlers stood up. "Take a look at my eyes,

will you, Doc?" He blinked his eyes. "I don't see very good this morning."

Doc pretended to examine the man's eyes. "Only thing the matter with your eyes, Pete, is that rotgut you drink. If you don't cut down on the booze, you're going to be dead by the time you're forty."

"Why, hell, Doc! I'm forty-five now!"

"See what I mean, boys?" Doc appealed. "Pete's been dead five years already and don't even know it."

Amid their laughter and whoops he strolled on down the street.

There were a few women shopping in the general store. The saloon keeper was unlocking his front door. A few early breakfasters were in the cafe. Bob Noel waved at Doc through the bank window. The undertaking establishment wasn't doing any early business and the night man at the livery stable was just going home.

For a moment Doc thought it was Bryce. Then he realized his mistake. The night man did look a lot like Bryce though. There was the same height and build. From a distance you could mistake one for the other. Their walking manner was similar. Doc went on with his stroll.

When he reached the end of the main street he turned in at the sheriff's office. Sid Harris, the deputy, was sweeping the floor. Sid didn't look anything like his boss the sheriff. Where Amos was long and lean, Sid was short and heavy set. His hair had thinned out and he had a large bald spot on the back of his head. He wore faded Levi's, scuffed boots, a neatly mended shirt, a badge, and a six-shooter in a well-worn holster. Sid's movements were slow and deliberate as he pushed the broom.

"Hello, Doc. Come in and set a spell. Can I get you some coffee?"

Doc dropped into a chair. "Sure can, Sid. I haven't had my second cup yet."

Sid propped his broom up in the corner and went over to the potbellied stove on which the coffee pot bubbled and filled a cup. "Are you making it all right, Doc?" he asked over his shoulder before he turned and handed Doc the cup of coffee.

"Don't really know, Sid. It's too early in the morning for me to be full awake yet, and I haven't been in town long enough to get back in the swing of things. I guess I'll make it."

Sid poured himself a cup of coffee. "I'm sure sorry about all your troubles, Doc." He pulled up another chair and sat down.

Doc nodded his head. "So am I."

The two men settled back in their chairs sipping their coffee and honored the early morning coffee drinking ritual with silence, though Doc's nerves were screaming. Would Sid back Amos' alibi? "Sid," Doc asked finally, "can you tell me something?"

Sid set his cup down on the arm of his chair but kept his grip on the handle. "What?"

"You remember the night of the party, the night Jeanne was killed? Amos said you came to report to him." Doc watched the deputy's face intently.

"Sure." The response was quick and certain. "I remember that night real well. I always report to Amos about 10 o'clock and I did then."

"Well," Doc's voice rose a little, "he also said that you two were standing out on the front porch when he heard me yelling in the library."

"That's where we were!" Sid's answer was emphatic. "I heard you, too."

Doc leaned forward in his chair, bringing his face closer to his companion's face. "Sid, this is mighty important. How long had you and Amos been standing on the front porch talking?"

Sid blinked, thought for a moment. "About fifteen minutes," he decided at last. "I'd been making the rounds and ran into a little trouble down at the saloon. Couple of the boys were full of likker and fight. I had to lock them up to get sober. Amos always wants to know who's in jail for the night and for why. It took me a while to tell him who our guests were that evening."

Doc held the deputy's eyes with his own. "You're sure then that Amos was on the front porch for at least fifteen minutes before he heard me shout?"

"Certain sure. You sounded like a banshee. Scared the hell out of both of us. We didn't waste any time getting to the library. Amos won that footrace. He got there a minute before I did."

That sounded authentic. At least that much of Amos' story checked out. If Sid wasn't lying to cover up for his boss. Tension drained out of Doc and he leaned back in his chair and took a sip of coffee.

"Anything else you need to know?" Sid asked.

Doc gave Sid a warm smile. "No, that's all I need. You've been a lot of help." He reached over and shook the deputy's hand.

"Glad to oblige. Want some more coffee?" Rising, Sid moved over to the stove.

Doc shook his head. "Thanks. I've had enough for one morning. Guess I better run along." Doc returned his cup to his host and started for the door. "See you around, Sid."

Doc walked out of the sheriff's office and cut across a couple of back lots to come up in the rear of the Noel house. Bob Noel was at the bank. No need for anyone in the house to know that Doc was calling on Delia. He could hear the cook singing in the kitchen as she went about her morning chores.

> Ho, Brother Teague, dost hear the degree,
> Lillibullero bullen a la.
> Dat we shall have a new deputy,
> Lillibullero bullen a la.

Doc was taken by surprise. He hadn't heard that song since his grandfather died. How the Irish cling to their songs! Two hundred years later, half a world away, and they still sing of a Protestant massacre.

He knocked lightly on the back door then stepped through into the kitchen.

"Why, Dr. Killian." Delia looked up from her stove. "And I'm proud to see you this fine morning! I heard you were come back. For good, I trust?" She held out her hand.

Doc shook it. "Yes, Delia. I've come home and this time I mean to stay."

"Would you be wanting a fresh-baked piece of bannock?"

"Thanks, Delia. That would be fine."

Delia returned to her oven and broke off a good-sized portion of bannock from a flat loaf that she had just removed from the fire. She put it on a plate, reached into her pantry for butter and jam, which she placed on the kitchen table, and signed for Doc to sit down. He sat at the table, picked up a knife, buttered the hot bannock, spread jam thickly on it, and took a bite.

"You haven't lost your touch, Delia. This is just as good as I remember."

Delia's plump, red face was wreathed in a smile as she settled in a chair across the table from Doc and studied him closely. They'd been friends for a long time.

When Doc finished eating he wiped his mouth with a napkin. "Delia, there's something I need to know. Do you remember the night of the party when Jeanne was killed?"

"Faith, I remember it as though it were yesterday." Delia crossed herself. "Your poor Jeanne. May her soul rest."

"At my trial Jim Balinte said that he was in your kitchen getting some paprika for his drink when he heard me shout from the library. Was he?"

Delia collected her thoughts and frowned as she recalled the events of that long ago night. "Yes, Doctor. The good Mr. Jim was with me at that moment. He'd come out to get some spice for his drink. Being the gentleman that he is, he insisted upon getting it himself so as not to be putting me to any bother."

"How long was he in the kitchen before he left?"

"I should think a good quarter of an hour, Doctor. He took time to tell me somewhat about the doings at the party and got his paprika. Yes, it was at least fifteen minutes, perhaps more."

That seemed to put Jim in the clear, if Delia had her time right.

Doc was glad. Glad that gentle Jim probably wasn't the

killer. Philosophers seldom make good murderers. They're too philosophic for one thing. Too compassionate for another.

Doc pushed his chair back. "Delia, it's been good, eating your baking and talking to you again. Now that I'm back home, we'll have to do it more often."

Delia rose from the table and started to clear away the dishes. "Anytime you want to come, you know you're more than welcome."

Doc left the Noel house the same way he'd come in. He traced his route through the back lots and came out on Main Street across from the sheriff's office. Amos Dalton was just about to go into his office when he looked across the street and saw Doc.

"Hey, Doc!" Amos yelled. "Come over here. I want to talk to you."

Doc crossed the street and both men went into the sheriff's office. Amos sat down at his desk and motioned for Doc to take a seat. Amos wet his lips. "I hear you been talking about me. I spoke to Sid just before he went home this morning and he said you'd been in to see him. He also said that you were asking questions as to my whereabouts the night of the murder."

Doc looked steadily at the sheriff. "Yes, Amos, I did."

There was a brief silence. Neither spoke till apparently Amos could stand it no longer. "Don't keep me in suspense. Why did you ask?"

"Sheriff," said Doc, "to my way of thinking there's a few unanswered questions about Jeanne's death."

"I didn't think there was." Amos rubbed his lean jaw. "The trial seemed pretty cut and dried. Have you come up with some new evidence I missed? Maybe you don't think I know how to do my job, but believe me, I do. I went over the Noel place with a fine-tooth comb. There was no sign of anyone except you being at the scene of the crime. And what the hell are you up to now? You've been over to see Delia."

"How did you know that?"

Amos shrugged his shoulders. "Where else would a man go if he was seen coming across the back lots in the direction of

Noel's house? Bob's at work in the bank this time of day. His wife's visiting her sister. Who else would you go to see?"

"Remind me to cover my tracks a little better next time, Sheriff."

"You better. If I can guess what you're doing, so can other folks. What did Delia say?"

"She told me that Jim is probably in the clear."

Amos jumped up from his chair and took a few steps around the office. "Just a minute, Doc! You mean to tell me that you've suspected both me and Jim of having killed your wife?" He came to a halt, staring down at his guest.

Doc nodded his head. "That's right, Amos. Not only you two; but also Bob, Bill, and Bryce."

Amos sat back down in his chair. "But that's crazy!"

"I'm sorry, Amos. That's what's been eating me for three years. I thought one of you five might have killed Jeanne. I still have my doubts. However, you and Jim seem to have alibis."

Amos was at a loss for words. "You really didn't do it?"

"I really didn't."

Amos gave a slow whistle. "No wonder you got mad at that card game. Then that just leaves three names on your suspect list: Bill, Bob, and Bryce. But why in hell did you suspect just the five of us and not someone else?"

"Amos, the night Jeanne died, all five of you were out of the ballroom at the same time. Any one of you could possibly have had the opportunity to kill her. Just why—I wouldn't know."

Amos scratched his head looking embarrassed and baffled. "So that's it. I didn't know about that. Why didn't you tell me?"

Doc shrugged. "Supposing you were the killer? All I could hope to do was come back and square things myself—if I didn't hang."

Amos put his hand on Doc's shoulder. "I'm sorry. Damned sorry! But it was your derringer fired the shot. It was you I found standing over Jeanne's body. It just looked so certain . . ."

"Yeah. Didn't it?" said Doc dryly.

The two men stared deep into each other's eyes. It was an electric moment. Doc could tell that the sheriff was turning the whole affair over in his lawman's brain. "I can see where you would be suspicious of the five of us. But it's mightly slim evidence. You mad at me 'cause I had to arrest you?"

"I don't hold it against you, Amos. Any peace officer would have done the same. Forget it."

"I'm sure not going to!" Amos vowed. "What are you going to do now?"

"I'm going to find out what Bill, Bob, and Bryce were doing the night Jeanne was killed."

"Sure you want to do that?"

Doc didn't think he'd heard right. "What do you mean?"

Amos gripped the arms of his chair. "I mean, why don't you let it go? You've already checked on Jim and me, we got good alibis. You'll probably find out that the other three have too. Could have been a total stranger. Why keep yourself all churned up over something that's over?"

For a moment Doc saw red. "Over?" he blazed. "Yes, Jeanne's life is over—and so are three years of mine! You tell me to forget it? Not while I'm breathing!"

"Doc—"

Swallowing, Doc got himself under control. "It's a matter of simple justice," he said more calmly. "A murder's been committed. Whoever did it must answer for it. How can civilization survive if we don't uphold the law? Surely you, as a sheriff, can understand that?"

"Doc, I understand what you're saying," Amos said carefully. "I also know that sometimes the law needs to be a little flexible. Whoever killed Jeanne has had to live with that for the same three long years that you were locked up at Yuma. A prison doesn't necessarily have to have bars on it to make it a real living hell of a prison."

Doc thought on what Amos had said. Then he quoted from memory: "Stone walls do not a prison make, nor iron bars a cage . . ."

"Something like that." Amos nodded. "Jeanne's killer will never know a moment's inner peace for the rest of his life."

"That may well be, Amos." Doc's hands clenched and he spoke between his teeth. "I still figure to track the killer down and bring him to my justice."

Amos watched him. At last he sighed. "That's really my job, Doc. You got no business trying to take the law into your own hands."

Doc got up from his chair. "Maybe so. Still, I'm going to talk around town and try to find out where my other three suspects spent their time when they were out of the ballroom. You don't happen to know?"

Amos rose from his chair and shook his head. "I don't. If you can convince me they're really suspects, I'll investigate myself."

Doc's face was grim. "I'll sure try, Amos. And if I find any other suspects I'll let you know."

Amos started over to his desk. "Doc, I just thought of something I was supposed to tell you. You remember Opal Johnson."

Opal's name turned over in Doc's memory. An image came to his mind of a tall, thin, pleasant-looking, kind of plain woman, who wore glasses. He also remembered the warmth of her smile and the easy companionship of her company. Opal was the sort of woman who put first-met strangers at their ease by her practical manner and good plain common sense. She was an easy woman to be with.

"You mean the schoolteacher. Sure, I remember her well."

The sheriff nodded. "That's the one. I saw her this morning on my early rounds. She asked me to tell you to drop by and see her when you found time. School lets out about three o'clock."

"O.K.," said Doc. "I'll go by and see her this afternoon. Thanks for talking with me. I'll let you know when I find out anything."

"You do that, Doc. Oh, by the way." Amos reached into his desk drawer and came up with a gun in his hand. It was Doc's derringer. The gun that had killed Jeanne. Amos handed the gun to Doc. "Thought you might like to have your gun back."

Doc looked at the gun. He saw it again, lying beside Jeanne as the blood pumped from her wound. A lump rose in his throat. He tried to swallow it and couldn't. Nodding his thanks, he put the gun in his hip pocket, stepped out of the office and started back up the street to return home.

He had lots of thinking to do. He could do it best in his own house. Settled in his favorite rocker, he was plagued by new questions. Why did Opie want to see him? He hadn't seen her for three years. Not since the night of the fatal party. No. That wasn't right. He'd last seen Opie when she came to visit him in jail. The memory of her kindness warmed him. But what about Opie at the party? She had been there. Alone because she was a widow. And yet, not alone. Opie attracted men because she could talk sense and didn't play the clinging vine like so many women did. But what was it he wanted to remember about their conversation that night? The answer refused to come.

Did Opie know something that would help in his search? Maybe Opie had the hint he needed to find Jeanne's killer.

He was sure going to go see Opie at three o'clock sharp.

Chapter 8

A few minutes before the courthouse clock struck three o'clock, Doc got his hat on and started for the schoolhouse. The building was located out at the edge of town on the opposite side of the courthouse from the main street. As Doc walked along, he passed a number of children on their way home from school. He knew most of them. He had either attended their births, or else doctored them for childhood ailments. They gave Doc a civil greeting, as was his due, being an adult. But none of them really were friendly as they had been in times past, and he winced when he caught some of them staring back at him and whispering.

Parents' attitudes were soon picked up by children. Doc wondered what lurid tales of murder those kids had heard about him. It was a wonder they didn't turn tail and run when they saw him coming. He must seem like an ogre to them.

Coming up even with the schoolyard fence, he paused a moment to think about Opie.

Immediately there came to his mind the memory of a warming smile. For an old maid schoolteacher Opie certainly had a pleasant, inviting look about her. Not that she was really an old maid. Doc was surprised he had never paid more attention to her in the past. She was well put together and quite attractive in her own way. He guessed that it had been the stereotyped schoolteacher image in his mind that had kept him from thinking about her as a desirable woman. That, and his being so wild about Jeanne.

Opie had been in Gila Crossing when Doc first arrived. A widow who had married a ne'er-do-well drunkard in her youth.

Her husband's name had been Eddie Johnson. He was a gambler as well as a drinker.

The late husband had managed to get himself killed in a saloon brawl. He had been drunk and abusive. A fellow boozer had knocked him down in a one-blow fist fight. When Opie's husband went down, he'd hit his head on the brass footrail below the bar and died of concussion. Opie was the only one in town who had mourned his death.

She'd never done anything else during her married life except work at two jobs. She taught school to support herself and her husband and was also a wife and housekeeper. Mercifully, she'd never had children. Most of the people of Gila Crossing considered Opie was better off a widow than she'd ever been as a married woman.

You never could have told how she really felt. In good times or in adversity, Opie was always the same: cheerful, even-tempered, a thoroughly nice person.

Doc tried to remember when they'd first met. He couldn't. Opie had always been in the background of his consciousness as long as he had been in Gila Crossing. She'd never been to see him as a patient. The only times she had ever been in his office was when she'd brought in a sick schoolchild or the ailing wife of one of the indigent families in town. Come to think of it, Opie had never asked Doc to do anything for herself. She was always after him to do something for someone else.

She was a self-contained woman who stood on her own two feet. The few times they had ever talked, she'd done all of the listening and he'd done all of the talking. She was the kind of woman who had the gift of drawing out a man's thinking and letting him express it in words. A rare quality in a woman.

Another thing Doc had forgotten was that on the night of the party at Noel's house she'd been pouring the punch. He had been flying a little higher than usual that night and Opie had been giving him only half a glass at a time. She'd even kidded him about drinking too much in such a nice way that he'd slowed down on his trips to the punch bowl. It was as though Opie had been warning him to keep his wits about him. Did she have reason to believe he'd need to be alert? Doc meant to find out.

He went through the gate, up the schoolhouse steps, entered the building. Opie sat at her desk in the front of the room correcting papers. She looked up as Doc entered and gave him a brief smile.

Opie Johnson was about five feet eight inches tall and probably weighed one hundred and twenty-five pounds. A trifle thin for Doc's tastes but she had pleasantly natural curves in all the right places. Her hair was light brown and she wore it swept back in a ponytail that flitted back and forth when she turned her head.

Her hands were graceful, tapered to long, thin fingers tipped with short fingernails. They looked like capable hands used to doing meaningful work. Doc liked what he saw in her.

"Hello, Doc." Opie pushed the papers aside. "Long time no see."

Doc gave her a wry grin. "Hello, Opie. I've been away."

"Yes, I know." Opie motioned for him to sit down. "How was it at Yuma?"

Doc squeezed himself into one of the desks. "Do you really want to know?"

Opie smiled one of her warm smiles that made Doc feel as though he were the only man in the world. "Yes, Doc. I really want to know. Tell me about it."

Opie's kind, light blue eyes met Doc's with such intensity that he felt as though he wanted to tell this woman everything he'd kept locked up in his mind for the last three years. A magnetic current seemed to flow between them. Doc opened the floodgates of his prison memories.

"Physically, it wasn't too bad." Doc felt somewhat like a schoolboy reciting his lessons. "I was never mistreated. Aside from Spartan living conditions, Yuma was pretty much like being in the Army. I had the good fortune to be assigned the job of prison doctor, had my own private room, and was a trustee. I had a certain amount of freedom of movement within the prison walls. During my off-duty hours I was even able to keep my hand in at playing poker. Mentally, though, it was pretty tough."

Doc fell silent. Opie came out from behind her desk and sat down beside him. Her physical closeness and the good, clean smell of her encouraged him to go on, free his mind.

"Opie, it was the most demeaning experience of my entire life. Not just being confined but the flogging of the spirit that degrades you to the status of an animal. Certain types of men, natural-born criminals if you will, thrive on prison life. They fit into the inmate hierarchy and prosper on the spoils system of the kangaroo court—but a man of spirit can only sicken in such surroundings. Each day of imprisonment, bending to the will of his keepers and the prison system, drives another nail into his spiritual coffin. A couple more years in Yuma and I'd have been a vegetable. Alive, but dead in all particulars that separate a man from an animal. Yet, I was one of the lucky ones. I had privileges the ordinary con is never granted. Even so, it was a soul-deadening experience and one that . . ."

Hell! Here he was blabbing his mouth and talking about his own problems even before he could ask her what she knew about the night of the murder and what life had done to her in the past three years. Evidently life had been good. She seemed calm and content.

"Go on. I'm listening." Opie touched his arm.

A small shock ran through Doc at her touch. "You listen too well, woman," he growled. "What's with you? What have you been doing while I was away?"

"Much the same." Opie spread her arms out and turned her hands upward. "Trying to teach the English language to incipient cowpokes and future ranch wives who won't ever really need to know any more than how to say: 'Whoa hoss' and 'Junior, yew hesh up thet thar cryin'.' Sometimes it seems like a hopeless task."

Doc laughed. "And yet you keep on trying?"

"Yes, I keep on trying. Because every so often a kid comes along who really wants to learn. A child who needs just a push in the right direction and you know that he or she will go on to bigger and better things in life than just living forever in a one-horse cow town. Sometimes it's pretty grim being a schoolmarm, but mostly I enjoy it."

Doc couldn't stand the cramped space of the school desk any longer. He stood up and stretched his legs. "Opie, I need to know something that maybe you can help me with."

Opie looked up at him. "What?"

"It's about the night that Jeanne got killed. You were there at the party and . . ."

"You were pretty drunk."

Doc grimaced. Yet he knew that Opie spoke the truth. If he hadn't spent so much time at the punch bowl, maybe, just maybe, Jeanne would be alive today.

"You're right, Opie. I was drunk."

Opie got up and went to stand beside him.

"No offense. It's just that I wanted to remind you that you weren't at your sharpest that night. In fact, you missed a number of things that you should have noticed earlier than you did."

"Like what?"

"For one thing, Doc, Jeanne left the ballroom about twenty minutes before you ever noticed she was gone and went looking for her. You were so busy drinking and talking to me that it's a wonder you missed her when you did. And another thing. All five of your men friends disappeared about the same time she did."

Once again Doc became aware of Opie's perceptive powers. "Here all these years I thought I was the only one who knew that."

"I knew it too, Doc."

"What else can you tell me that I might have missed?"

Opie hesitated. "I've debated with myself for three years about whether or not to tell you this, but I think you ought to know. Jeanne left the ballroom with Bryce."

Doc's stomach turned and tied itself into little knots. Bryce again! Could it be that Bryce had managed to fascinate Jeanne? Had they gone off for a tryst in the library?

No! Doc wouldn't believe that! Had Bryce lured Jeanne into a compromising position and then shot her when she resisted his advances? This came closer to probability. Why would Bryce shoot her? A man of his womanizing character wouldn't kill a woman just because she spurned him. No, it had to be something more than that. Something deeper, heavier than a party flirtation. Doc wished he knew more about Jeanne's past life before they met. There had to be some connection between Jeanne's death and her past. What it might be, Doc had not the slightest idea.

"I know what you must be thinking," said Opie, "but I don't think Bryce had anything to do with Jeanne's death."

"How can you say that?" asked Doc. "You just told me they left the party together."

"They did. But Bryce was only gone about ten minutes when he came back around to the side of the house. I could see him outside the ballroom window smoking a cigar. You were too pie-eyed to notice him standing there about fifteen minutes before you shouted from the library." Opie gave her head an emphatic shake that made her ponytail bounce. "No, I don't think Bryce did it."

Doc wasn't ready to be convinced of Bryce's innocence. Of course, Opie could be right. If, as she said, Bryce had been standing outside for fifteen minutes before Doc started yelling, then he must have left Jeanne a good quarter of an hour before she was killed. A recently fired gun doesn't smoke for that long a time. Bryce could be in the clear.

Funny how you always tend to suspect a good-looking man of any devious thing that happens. Must be male envy, this distrust of a handsome man. It was just as likely that a homely man was guilty—must have gone clear back to the days of the cavemen when the most well-endowed male garnered the most desirable females and the lesser males made do with what was left. It was an unfair attitude, but it persisted.

The mere fact that Bryce had left the party with Jeanne would mean that he was the next to last person to see her alive. If he wasn't the killer.

And what of the other two men, Bill and Bob? The hunt was narrowing. Doc's nerves tautened and his inside knotted. Soon he'd have to decide who, among his friends, he would have to go after. He hadn't found any other evidence pointing to any other suspects. It almost had to be one of them.

It was like the end of a javelina hunt when the dogs had run down all but the strongest and most dangerous of the boars. This end boar would be the most cunning and deadly. He was the one dogs and hunters had better fear, the one with nothing to lose and everything to gain by a sudden assault on those who were about to bring him down.

Doc's enemy would have the advantage of knowing what Doc didn't. That he was the hunted one. Doc had to move softly, try not to alert the guilty man.

Maybe Bryce could throw some light on the mystery. He seemed to have been the next to last person to see Jeanne alive. The last person was the killer. Doc must talk to Bryce and learn all he knew about what had happened. Some apparently insignificant detail might supply the needed clue.

"Opie," Doc said, "thanks for telling me about Bryce. He's been a sure enough suspect on my list. You've just saved me lots of legwork."

"What about the other four men?" Opie played absently with a curl of soft brown hair. "Amos and Jim both had an alibi at the trial. Did you check their stories?"

"Yes. Their stories checked out with reliable witnesses. I'm pretty sure about their whereabouts when Jeanne was killed." Doc tried sitting at the pupil's desk again, but he was too big and had to stick his feet and legs out in the aisle.

"Then that leaves you Bill and Bob?"

"Yes, Opie. I don't know about those two. Do you know where they were when Jeanne was killed?"

Opie shook her head. "I was talking to you and watching Bryce through the window. I don't have any idea where the other two went. I'll ask around with my women friends. Of all the people who were at the party, surely someone will · remember. I'll send word out on the gossip line and see what I can come up with. In the meantime, you might just have your-self a little talk with the three friends you believe in and see what they know about the other two."

Doc shifted position to give his legs more room. "Amos doesn't seem to know anything except what he told at the trial. I'll see Jim and Bryce just as soon as I can."

"That's a place to start," approved Opie. "In the meantime, I'll keep my eyes and ears open. But be careful. You've got a lot of living to make up."

Doc got to his feet. "Well, thanks again Opie. Guess I better let you finish your papers."

Opie motioned for him to sit back down. She wasn't through with him yet. "The papers can wait. Schoolteachers never get to the end of all the papers. It's one of the rules of the game that as soon as you finish one batch, you get another. Pupils' papers are an endless chain that go on forever, supply a continuity to life. Do you need a batch of papers, Doc?"

"What do you mean by that?" Doc was puzzled.

"I mean that life goes on. Life is for the living. When are you going to start living again?"

"Why, I'm living right now, Opie."

"Are you?" Opie snorted the question. "Aren't you so wrapped up in your search for vengeance you've forgotten what it's like to be alive?"

Doc was slightly miffed. "One thing at a time. I'm going to find Jeanne's killer and bring him to justice. That's the whole point of my existence right now."

"All right"—Opie grimaced—"you're set on finding the mur-derer. What if you don't? What if you check out Bill and Bob and neither is the killer? What if you never learn who killed Jeanne? What of your life then?"

Doc considered Opie for several seconds. She was driving at something deeper than the surface meaning of her words.

"Opie, are you trying to tell me something? You better spell it out for me because I'm just a poor old country boy who doesn't understand a lot of things."

Opie's face turned beet-red. She glanced away, biting her

lips. And then, making a quick decision that went against the grain of what society expected of a woman, she blurted out what was on her mind.

"What I'm trying to tell you, you damned fool, is that you're a man and I'm a woman. I'm alive and Jeanne's dead. It's as simple as that."

Doc was nonplussed. In all his past experience he had never run across a woman as blunt as Opie. It had been so many years since he'd been an eligible male that he'd almost forgotten the rituals of courtship. The very idea of a woman finding him attractive kind of scared him. For the first time he looked at Opie, considering her as a woman, not just an interesting person who'd been his friend at a friendless time.

His steady gaze seemed to fluster her, but doggedly she went on. "You never have thought of me as being a woman, have you?" she accused. "Did the thought ever occur to you that I've been a widow longer than you've been a widower?"

She looked away. Her words came hesitantly but with insistence. "I'm a woman, Doc. I have needs and wants and desires that need fulfilling. I think you could do that for me." Her voice quivered, but she continued bravely.

"That's what I mean about living. You're so tied up with your past and grieving for a dead wife, you haven't given yourself a chance to act like a man again." She paused as though building up her courage to say more.

"I need a man and you need a live woman. What's living without a desire to share your life with another person?"

She turned as if unable now to face him. Thoroughly uncomfortable, Doc pulled out his handkerchief and wiped his brow. "Opie, you kind of overwhelm me! I'm so mixed up I don't know what to say. I guess I haven't thought about what I'm going to be doing the rest of my life. I need time to think these things through."

"Take all the time you need, fellow. You've got all the time in the world. Why, you can't be more than forty-two or forty-three years old."

Opie was joshing him but at the same time reminding Doc of her own sense of urgency about their relationship.

Doc answered her seriously. "I'm fifty years old."

Opie squinted an eye at him. "Like I said before. Take your time. You've got years of life left. Come on. Let's get out of school for the day. If you're not scared of what the gossips will say," Opie looked at him archly, "I'll even let you walk me home." The color still had not left her cheeks. But she had said her piece.

They walked out of the schoolhouse. While Opie locked the front door, Doc noticed a fresh set of bootprints in the dust of the yard. The tracks led up to the side window close to where Doc and Opie had been sitting inside. They then turned and went around back of the schoolhouse and trailed off into the mesquite bushes. They were not child-sized bootprints.

Somebody had been eavesdropping on their conversation. Doc wondered how long the person had been outside the window and what he'd overheard. Maybe it was just some nosy townsman who wanted some grist for the morning gossip mill. If the interloper had heard Opie speak out, the tongues would fairly clack themselves sore tonight.

Doc grinned wryly, admiring Opie's courage in going against all the conventions and saying what she wanted.

Quite a woman was Opie. No beauty like Jeanne but good to be with. Comforting yet bracing. Doc stared again at the bootprints.

What if it had been Jeanne's killer listening? If so, the hunted was warned, might this minute be planning an ambush. Doc felt the short hairs on the back of his neck stand up.

From now on he had to be mighty careful. Or else he wouldn't get the justice his heart demanded; and direct, funny, valiant Opie would have to look around for another man.

Chapter 9

Opie finished locking up the schoolhouse and came down the steps to join Doc. "What do you find so fascinating about footprints?" she asked.

"This particular set indicates that someone was listening to our little conversation."

Opie's face flushed. "Oh! I'm sorry! What I said in there—I didn't mean for anyone else to hear. I just wanted to level with you."

"So you can still blush, can you?" Doc laughed though the situation might not be funny. "I didn't think you were still that young."

Opie did a fast pirouette. "There's a dance or two in the old girl yet. A woman's as old as she looks; but a man's old when he stops looking."

Doc stroked the gray hairs at his temple. "I'm not that old—yet." He took her arm. She looked startled, then pleased as they left the schoolyard and walked to her house. At the front stoop, Doc grinned at her and stuck out his hand. "Give her a shake, pardner?"

Opie grinned back and grasped his hand firmly. "O.K. this time, pardner. But I don't want you to think I'm the kind of girl who does this with every fellow on their first date. When I really like a guy, I let him kiss me. I like you, Doc."

"Opie! I swear to God. You're the most forward woman I ever met."

"God helps those who help themselves," said Opie. "Where are you going now?"

"Down to see Bryce at the livery stable." Doc paused,

watched her till she colored again. "Thanks for the conversation. Some of it was right interesting." He moved on.

As he drew even with her front gate Opie called, "One more
platitude, Doc."

He turned and faced her. "What's that?"

"Time heals all wounds. I know. I've been there."

Doc nodded. But no matter what anyone said, only justice
would heal his angry, aching wounds. "I hope you're right." He
threw her a salute with his hand. "I'll see you around."

"You can make book on that." Opie went through her front
door and into the house.

Doc set a course for the livery stable, turning over in his
mind the things Opie had told him. The more he thought
about her directness, the more amused he became. Finally, he
burst out laughing and stood stock still in the middle of the
road until the fit left him. Man alive! You knew where you
stood with a woman like Opie! But he knew very well she'd
never have talked like that unless she cared about him. He
wasn't sure he was worth her concern. Maybe he was so eaten
up with the urge for revenge that he was scarcely a man anymore. A man who could treat her right.

The livery stable was located about halfway down the main
street of Gila Crossing. It had a clapboard false front that rose
two stories high. All across the high front of the building was a
sign that said Collins Livery Stable.

There was a large window and a door on the left side of the
building where Bryce's office was located. A wide archway in
the center of the front allowed access for horses, wagons, and
buggies. The right-hand side of the building front was solid.
Looking through the archway, Doc could see an open stable
yard surrounded by stalls. He peered through the office window
but could see no one inside. Stepping through the archway he
continued through the stable yard until he found Bryce mucking manure out of one of the stalls.

"At last I know what you're good for," said Doc.

Bryce paused in his pitchforkng and grinned. Then he solemnly handed over his fork. "My dear fellow, I'm a rank ama-

teur. Please feel free to demonstrate the proper technique."

Doc took the proffered tool and swung a few loads out of the stall onto a manure pile. "That's how you do it, me lad. See if you can't do better in the future."

Bryce took the fork back. "Thanks for the lesson. Usually I feel that virtue is its own reward, but in your case I'll pay off with a drink. Come in my office and I'll stand you a slug of red eye."

The two men went into Bryce's office and sat down. Bryce reached into his lower desk drawer, pulled out a bottle of Bourbon, two glasses, and poured out two shots. "Here's to wives and sweethearts sweet—may they never, never meet," toasted Bryce.

"I'll drink to that," said Doc. They drained their glasses.

"What's on your so-called mind?" questioned Bryce. "I know you didn't come down here just to drink my whiskey. Of course, if you were one of the gentler sex," Bryce leered at Doc, "I might lay your interest to my fatal fascination."

"In a way my visit does have to do with your fascination with and for women," said Doc straight-faced. "I just talked to Opie. She says you left the ballroom with my wife the night she was killed."

Bryce looked at Doc through half-slitted eyes and braced himself in his chair. His muscles tensed as he leaned forward. Doc hurried to put him at his ease.

"Relax, Bryce. Opie also told me that you left Jeanne about ten minutes later and were standing where she could watch you about the time Jeanne died. All I want to know is what happened during the ten minutes you were with Jeanne."

Bryce let his breath out and settled back in his chair. "For a minute you had me worried. I've had a few unpleasant experiences with angry husbands in my time. I'll be glad to tell you what Jeanne and I were up to when we left the ballroom."

Doc put his glass down. "I'm listening."

"Nothing." Bryce shrugged.

Doc leaned forward. "What do you mean, nothing?"

"Exactly that. I had been dancing with Jeanne. The music

ended. You were at the punch bowl talking to Opie. Jeanne said she wanted to go to Noel's library to find a book of poems. Seems like the music had reminded her of some poetry that she'd almost forgotten. She said she wanted to refresh her memory. I walked with her to the library. When she found the book she was looking for, she told me she wanted to be alone for a little while to read her poem. That's all there was to it."

Doc considered Bryce's story. It was plausible. Jeanne was an avid reader. Her tastes ran to classics and poetry. She often sought out books at odd hours and moments when a certain thought or memory prompted. Odd, though, that she should have left a dance party to go seeking a poem.

"Do you know the name of the poem?" asked Doc as Bryce poured them another drink.

"Can't say I do." Bryce pushed the glass over to Doc. "You know I don't know anything except horses."

Doc took the full glass in his hand. "And women."

Bryce picked up his own drink. "Yes. You might say I know a little about them too."

"Was there anyone around the library when you left Jeanne?"

"Not a soul." Bryce worked on his whiskey. "I went out through the french doors and came on around the house. Didn't pass anybody on the way. I was standing outside of the ballroom window when you set up your ruckus."

"Do you have any idea who killed Jeanne? Would you have a notion where Bill and Bob were when it happened?"

"The answer to the first question is no, and the second's the same. Why do you ask about Bill and Bob?"

"Because I think one of them might be the murderer."

Bryce slammed his glass down. "Now, Doc. That's a hell of a thing to say. Why suspect those two guys? Why not Amos, or Jim—or even me?"

"Because I've already checked you out. Also Jim and Amos. I've pretty well accounted for where you three were that night. So far I haven't found out where the other two disappeared to when Jeanne was killed."

"I don't know either. But I sure wish you'd let this drop. Hell. I guess you can't." Bryce reached for the bottle. "Want some more whiskey?"

"No." Doc held up his hand. "Two drinks is my limit for one evening. How's the livery stable business these days?"

Bryce poured himself another shot. His hand shook a little. Evidently he was getting to be a heavier drinker than Doc had remembered him to be.

"Couldn't be better," said Bryce gaily. "I'm the only game in town. If anybody wants to travel, they have to come to me. I get a few drummers that come in on the stage. Mostly it's the local trade that keeps me in whiskey."

Doc remembered something he wanted to ask Bryce. "Your night man. What's his name?"

"Frank Kimbrough. Why do you ask?"

"He looks and acts enough like you to be your brother," opined Doc.

"He is kind of like a kid brother," observed Bryce. "He hired on with me a month or so before you went to Yuma. Hasn't got any parents. Kind of adopted me." Bryce chuckled. "He hasn't copied me completely. He's married."

"How come you never married, Bryce?"

"Why buy a cow when milk's so cheap?"

Doc snorted. "That's a half-assed reason. When you get too old to go catting around, you'll wish you had some companionship."

Bryce smiled ruefully. "I probably will, Doc."

"Hasn't there ever been a woman you wanted to tie up with?"

Bryce weighed his answer. "Yes. There was one woman once. Like most of my women—she was married."

"What became of her?"

"She died."

A silence fell over their conversation. They both mused over their own thoughts. Doc felt a new kinship to Bryce. They had both loved women who were dead. This was a side of Bryce

that Doc had never explored. It was a touchy subject. One better left alone.

Doc swirled the dregs of his whiskey around in the bottom of
his glass. "Bryce, what do you think happened on the night
Jeanne was killed?"

Bryce's face clouded over, he poured himself some more red
eye, shot the drink home, and stared up at the ceiling.
"Damned if I know."

Doc set his glass down. "Don't you have any theory about
how it happened? Can you think of anything you saw that
night that was out of the ordinary?"

"The only thing I can figure," Bryce's voice was a whisper,
"is that some perfect stranger busted into the library and killed
her accidentally. There's no reason why anyone would want to
kill Jeanne otherwise. She was one of the finest women ever to
walk the face of the earth." A tear came to his eye and ran
down his cheek.

Doc decided he'd better end the conversation right there. He
got up and stretched. "Guess I better get on home." He
yawned. "Thanks for the booze. It's made me sleepy." He went
to the door.

Bryce remained seated. "Good night, Doc. If you ever need a
horse of a different color, come around. I've several to choose
from."

Doc nodded his thanks and went out the office door. Evening was falling fast and he did feel sleepy. He started up the
main street towards his house. Coming down the street from
the other direction he saw Frank Kimbrough going to work.

Frank was about the same size as Bryce. Maybe an inch
shorter and a few pounds lighter. He wore his hair long, parted
in the middle and swept back around his ears in graceful curves
that were almost a carbon copy of Bryce's hair style. As they
started to pass one another Doc said: "Hello, Frank."

"Hello, Dr. Killian." Frank's voice was fairly high pitched. "I
didn't know you knew my name."

Doc gestured towards the livery stable. "I've been talking to
Bryce. He told me who you are."

"I hope Mr. Collins gave you a good report on me," Frank said earnestly.

"Oh, he did." Doc assured him as he started on down the street. "Good night, Frank."

Frank's light voice floated out on the night air. "Good night, Doctor."

As Doc walked on his mind was crowded with the things he had learned that day. First of all, Opie. She really seemed to like him. On the surface of things that didn't hardly make sense.

Doc was no lady's man. He was fifty years old. Had a full head of hair and most of his teeth. True, the hair had receded a bit from his younger days, but it still covered his head. His belt line had pushed out quite a bit in the last three years. Too much sitting and not enough bending over. Most of his contemporaries suffered from the same problem.

He'd never been handsome, but he wasn't ugly. His face was lined but mostly with fine laugh wrinkles around his eyes and mouth. When he was fresh shaven and dressed up he was as passable as any other fifty-year-old man. First thing in the morning, though, he looked and felt his age. At least that was his opinion. It seemed Opie saw him in a different light.

No accounting for a woman's taste in men. Some of the best-looking women married plain men. It didn't seem to matter much what a man looked like on the outside. Most women seemed to have a sixth sense that attracted them to the one man who was right for them.

In Opie's case her first husband must have had some qualities deep down inside that were never apparent to the outside world. Maybe it was the same way with her feeling for Doc. He guessed men seldom thought about women having inclinations of their own. Women were supposed to play a passive part and hardly ever express their own feelings. It was always for the male to dominate and make known his needs.

With Opie it would be a toss-up to see who was the dominant party in any relationship. She was so straightforward and open that any man who wanted to run in double harness with her would have to accept her as an equal. And, come to think of it, that wouldn't be such a bad way to travel. Opie could pull her own share of the load.

What was it Opie had said about the purpose of life? She had said there was more to living than a blind search for vengeance. Her concept had to do with sharing your life with another person. Maybe she was right. But first he had to settle that old score. Once that was done, maybe, just maybe he could live again.

Doc also thought about what he had learned by talking to Bryce. Bryce had been able to account for all except the last fatal minutes of Jeanne's life. It was up to Doc to account for those last ten minutes somehow.

Somehow he was going to have to find out where Bill and Bob fit into the picture. There had to be a way to put one of those men at the scene of the crime. And if they both had alibis like the other three friends, then Doc would have to reconsider all their stories—or find another suspect.

When Doc finally got to his house, he found a note stuck in his front door. The note was addressed to him in a very feminine handwriting. He took it out of the crack in the front door and went on into the house to light a lamp and read the note. Doc sat down in his easy chair to read the message. It was from Opie.

"Dear Doc," the epistle began, "I ran into Jim Balinte's wife, Betty, after you left me this evening. Betty told me, among other things, that Jim had some information about Jeanne that you would probably want to know. Why don't you go see Jim tomorrow? Don't forget what I told you. Time wounds all heels. Opie."

Doc smiled at the pun. It was so like Opie to try and cheer him up when she knew his spirits would be low over learning something new about his dead wife.

Suddenly there was a splintering crash. Glass shattered and sprinkled through the air. Doc felt the sharp-edged debris digging into his scalp. The air stirred as the bullet whirred past his head and struck the opposite wall. He fell sideways out of his

chair, hit the floor. Shaking, he reached up, snuffed out the
reading lamp and sank close to the floor. Every muscle in Doc's
body trembled. No other sound broke the silence of the night.

Doc took a deep breath and made his unwilling legs respond.
He scrambled to his feet and ran for the front door. Instinctively he kept low as he moved past the window through which
the shot had come.

He gulped several more deep breaths into his quivering
lungs. Steeling his nerves, he grasped the front-door handle.
Heart thudding, he jerked the door wide while protecting his
body behind the door jamb.

The dark seemed inky black. Palm sweating on the door handle, he listened intently, but all he could hear was the pounding of blood in his ears.

As his eyes became accustomed to the change in light, he
could make out the dusty expanse of street in front of his
house. There was no one in sight. Doc cautiously stuck his
head through the doorway, scanned both directions.

No motion. No sound. Yet someone had been there a minute ago.

Someone with a gun who'd found a perfect lamplit target
framed in a house window. Doc's spine crawled and he broke
out in chill perspiration. Another inch in the other direction
and the bullet would have put an end to all his searching. The
tiniest error had spared Doc's life.

Or had it? Doc scowled. Most men on the frontier were better shots than that. Not too many would miss a stationary target at a distance of fifty feet. Doc gazed around, still listening,
but he was sure his attacker was gone. Had the miss been inten-
tional? Maybe the shot had been a warning that he was asking
too many questions, that he'd better leave the past alone. Doc
grunted, ran his tongue over his dry lips.

Well, he wasn't through! And he wasn't quitting.

But he was going to have to be damned careful. No more
presenting himself as a target, walking without fear of danger.
The hunted had turned hunter. Somehow he'd learned that
Doc was after him.

Doc went back into the house and closed the door. Stepping gingerly across the glass-scattered floor through the front room, he went into his bedroom and lit a lamp. He rummaged under some clothing in his top dresser drawer and came up with the .41 caliber derringer.

The gun that had killed Jeanne. Her wedding gift to him. The gun that Amos had just returned to him this morning. Before going to meet Opie at the schoolhouse, he had placed the gun in his drawer. He hadn't guessed he'd need it so soon.

The smooth curve of the mother-of-pearl handle fit snugly in his palm, the cold metal of the barrel steadying his jagged nerves. He broke the gun to check its load. The ends of two massive brass cartridges protruded from the firing chambers.

Doc snapped the gun back together. He was ready!

Chapter 10

Doc was up before dawn. The first thing he did was dig the slug out of the front-room wall. The bullet had hit a metal hinge plate and splintered into fragments that made it impossible to tell from what kind of gun it had been fired. Sighting backwards from the hole in the wall, through the broken windowpane, the angle of entry told Doc the shot had been fired from the vacant lot kitty-corner across from the front of his house.

It was an ideal spot for an ambush. Mesquite and ironwood formed dense cover where an assassin could wait until a target showed. Doc's spine tingled and his guts twisted as he remembered the hiss of the bullet, the shattering of glass.

He wasn't going to set himself up for potshots again.

Doc made himself hash-browned potatoes with two eggs broken on top, coffee liberally laced with cream and sugar, two slices of bread fried in the same skillet as the eggs and potatoes. All the food went on one plate.

Total dishes to be done: one skillet, one spatula, one cup, one plate; one each of knife, fork, and spoon. The coffee pot was left on the stove and kept warm the rest of the day. Doc liked to keep housekeeping chores to a minimum, but he didn't mind them. He'd married Jeanne for her mind, not for a cook and housekeeper, though she'd filled those roles very well.

One flip of his wrist swung the coverlet in place on the bed. He picked up the derringer off the dresser and put it in his hip pocket. He'd never carried a gun routinely but for a while one would be a pretty basic item of attire.

Now for Jim Balinte. Doc got out Opie's note and read it again, smiled once more at her pun.

Jim Balinte's place of business was located between the general store and the livery stable. At this early hour the place wasn't open. The one-story adobe with a clapboard false front had a large many-paned window in the front wall that served as a display case.

Inside the window was an open casket. Jim sold only quality merchandise and always had one of his best models on display. This particular one was upholstered with shiny white satin on the inside and covered with a soft gray fabric on the outside. Bright brass handles and a blank nameplate completed the hardware fittings. Very few of the local citizens ever took their last ride in such an elaborate contraption. It was strictly a display piece. Probably the only one of its kind in the territory.

Most of the departed made do with simpler wooden boxes. Jim kept a good selection in the storage room at the back. The display casket was his way of pointing out the vanity of man. Many bereaved gazed with wonder at the elegant beauty of this exquisite piece of craftsmanship, but upon learning its cost, the next of kin invariably decided that there was no need for the deceased to take it all with him.

Jim never really intended to sell his prize casket. He sometimes told his friends that he was saving it for himself.

"When I go," Jim was fond of saying, "I want to go in style. There'll be little enough for men to remember me by. Let them at least remember me as being a man who wasn't penurious when patronizing his own profession."

It was an excusable indulgence. Since Jim bought his supplies at wholesale, his fancy funeral would cost little more than the price of an ordinary burying.

Doc sat down on the boardwalk steps and waited for Jim to open up for the day. As he waited, he observed the morning stirrings of Gila Crossing.

The cafe was doing a land-office business. Mostly men. Many businessmen. Doc wondered if the more affluent townsmen ever ate breakfast at home. The cafe was more of a private club than a restaurant. Much town business was done at this place. Deals were made, prices established, livestock traded, and news circulated at these early morning gatherings.

Doc had never taken much part in them. He was a gregarious man by nature, but not first thing in the morning. The cycle of his life force was geared to late evening hours. Many a night he would sit up reading or thinking until dawn. Although he kept regular hours and rose as early as anyone else, Doc's mind never functioned at full tilt until noon or later. For the first few hours of the day he liked to be alone.

Since his return from prison, he'd been following the pattern of early rising forced on him at Yuma. Now that he was free again, he could enjoy the luxury of staying in bed a little later in the morning. That is, he would, once he solved the mystery of Jeanne's murder. Till that was done he wasn't going to sleep very well anytime—especially since the killer seemed to be after him.

Doc hadn't long to wait before Jim Balinte came down the boardwalk. Like most cavalrymen, Jim didn't walk very well. He'd spent too many years in the saddle to be at home on foot. His short, bowed legs swung him along in a series of rather awkward steps. He lurched rather than walked.

"Howdy stranger," grinned Jim. He reached in his pocket for his key. "They say the early bird catches the worm, but I never did like worms. You caught any?"

"Only one." Doc rose, stretched, and smiled at his friend. "You're my first catch this morning."

"C'mon inside. I'll get my tape and measure you up for a box. You hankering for that gray job in the window?"

"Got better things to spend my money on than making you rich. Besides, you'd look better wearing that one than I would."

"It's a matter of taste," Jim laughed. "Some guys have class and others don't care! Had your second cup?"

"Not yet."

"I'll put the pot on." Jim turned to the stove, thrust a few sticks of kindling in the firebox, and lit it with a match. He put fresh water in the pot, added a handful of coffee, got out two cups, and pulled up a chair opposite Doc.

"My wife tells me you've been talking to Opie."

"Yep."

"Interesting conversation?"

"Yep."

Jim clasped chubby hands over his ample midsection. "Old Hungarian proverb says: 'Man who says yep, has many other words he wants to say.' Of course, the yep loses something in translation."

"Jim, Opie wrote me a note last night and said you'd turned up something about Jeanne's death. What was it?"

"What I know isn't much." Jim fingered his goatee. "In fact, it's such a small thing that I didn't pay much attention to it right off. After the trial, after you went to Yuma, I began to put one and one together and figured out what that little detail meant."

A little late in the day. Doc fought to keep irony out of his voice.

"And what was the little detail?"

"Jeanne had a welt on her finger."

Doc frowned. "I don't follow you."

"She had a crease on her trigger finger like maybe she'd had tight hold of a gun." Jim pantomimed an outstretched gun hand, then turned it quickly toward himself. "The skin was scratched a bit like it would be if the gun had been shoved around real hard and quick in her hand."

"When I found her the gun was laying on the floor," Doc protested.

"Nevertheless, the mark on Jeanne's finger indicated to me that she was holding the gun when it was fired."

The scene in the Noel library came back to Doc's mind with sickening clarity. Jeanne on the floor. The smoking gun beside her. His own helplessness.

"Then you think Jeanne pulled the gun on somebody and that person forced the gun around so that she shot herself?" Doc asked softly.

Jim's broad face was somber. "That's the way it looks. It's not much to go on, but the finger mark couldn't have been made in any other way. When it dawned on me, I figured you'd still provoked her into drawing the gun and were guilty even though the actual shooting was accidental. Forgive me, Doc. I—I wasn't thinking very straight."

A surge of bitterness welled up in Doc. He let it wash through him, was surprised that it subsided in a few minutes.

"Past is past," he said. "This is a real clue, Jim! I'm glad Jeanne didn't give up without a struggle. It makes me feel a little better to know she died fighting."

"It's a grim kind of consolation." Jim's kind eyes touched Doc sympathetically. "That's all I can tell you. I wish there was more."

He got up and hefted the coffee pot to pour their drinks. He gave Doc some sugar but took his own black. "Whoever killed Jeanne must have had an argument with her, frightened her so much that she went for her gun. A strong, quick man could easily turn the gun and cause her to shoot herself."

Doc stared at his coffee cup. His mind fleshed out pictures of the scene Jim had just described.

"It may have been an accident," Jim ventured. "Maybe the killer thought she was going to shoot him and slapped the gun away to protect himself. I can't to this day imagine anyone really wanting to kill Jeanne. How did she happen to have a gun at the party?"

"I wish I knew, Jim. I never knew her to carry a weapon. That derringer was her wedding present to me." Doc swallowed some coffee to settle the lump in his throat. "The last time I saw it, before the killing, it was in my dresser drawer. I never carried the weapon and neither did she—to my knowledge."

Doc sipped slowly, framing words in his mind before he spoke. "She must have known that something might happen the night of the party. I've wondered about maybe there being something in her past life that would explain what happened that night." He hesitated, pulse throbbing savagely, hating the question, dreading an answer, but driven to have it. "Do you was thinking I might need my gray box prematurely. And what about the rest of the Inside Straight Flush Weekly Sewing Circle?"

Doc grinned at Jim's old name for the poker group. "So far I've checked out you, Amos, and Bryce. Your alibis all seem to hold up. That just leaves Bill and Bob. But there's one thing I know for sure."

"What's that, Doc?"

"Somebody threw hot lead at me last night." Doc took the bullet fragments from his pocket and laid them in the palm of Jim's hand. "I was sitting in my lighted front room reading Opie's note when this little gem came whistling through the air. At first I thought it might have been some literary critic's comment on the note. Then I second-guessed that it was meant for me. Don't suppose you can guess what kind of gun it might have come from?"

Jim examined the lead pieces with the keen eye of a coroner. "No, I don't. Bullet fragments don't tell you much. Why would anyone be shooting at you?"

"That's the odd part about it, Jim. They were shooting at me. The range was too close and the target too well lit for them to miss. They were evidently trying to scare me off."

"Did they scare you?"

"Hell, yes!" Doc felt cold again in the pit of his stomach. "But not enough to make me quit asking questions or looking for answers."

Jim's pudgy hand gripped Doc's. "A brave man has fears and acts in spite of them. Only a fool can be fearless in the face of a situation that would scare the pants off a normal man. Where did the shot come from?"

"I must be getting senile!" Doc slapped his leg and spilled his coffee. "The shot came from that vacant lot across the street from my place. When I got up this morning I dug the slug out of the wall and then plumb forgot to look for tracks in the vacant lot. Want to come along while I cut for sign?"

"Might's well. Don't seem to be nobody dying to get into my place this morning."

know anything about Jeanne, before she met me, that might explain things?"

Jim considered, gave a heavy shrug. "Jeanne was a beautiful woman. She attracted men, liked men. She was the belle of many a ball before you came along. But I can't remember hearing that she was mixed up seriously with any man before your time. She could have been, though."

Doc shook his head. It had begun to ache with torturing insistence. "How can a man live with a woman for three years and still not know much about her? Jeanne once told me she'd been in Gila Crossing a little over two years before I came. Did she have a steady beau during that time?"

"Not real steady, Doc." Jim stumped over to the stove for more coffee. "She went around with first one fellow and then another, dated Bryce a few times. She never seemed to care much for any one man—until you came along."

Doc sipped his coffee and thought of her. If what Jim thought was true, then Jeanne had never been emotionally tied to anyone else.

But she could have had a secret affair, one no one guessed about. Had she broken off a romance with some man when she met Doc. If she had, there'd have been some reason for killing her.

Jeanne had never hinted such a thing to him, but Doc was increasingly sure there had to be something like that in Jeanne's past. He could think of no other motive for her death. Any man who'd loved her would have tried to keep her, maybe even killed her in despair at his loss.

"Am I still one of your suspects?" asked Jim. "A certain Irish songbird confessed to having conversed with you recently about my esteemed person. You should know you can't go anyplace in a small town like Gila Crossing without it being common knowledge. What's the verdict?"

"You, old man, will probably live to be hanged as a horse thief."

Jim nodded his head and his goateed chin resembled a woodpecker's bill delving for insects. "Glad to hear you say that. I

They finished their coffee and set out for the vacant lot. When they reached the spot from where Doc calculated the shot must have been fired, they found a set of boot tracks. Doc studied them, then turned to Jim. "I've seen these tracks before."

Jim gave him a quizzical look. "I thought you just told me back at my place that you forgot to check for prints this morning."

"I did, but I've seen these boot marks before."

Jim frowned slowly. "Let me in on your little secret."

"Yesterday I was at the schoolhouse. Opie and I talked a spell. When we came out of the school, I by chance noticed a set of tracks, just like these, where someone had listened by the window. Notice how the print of the right boot heel blurs on the outside edge? Whoever made this track, and the ones I found under the window, wears a boot with the right heel run down."

Jim looked thoughtful. "You're sure about the tracks being the same?"

"Real sure, Jim. I may not be the best tracker in the world, but I swear these prints and those at the schoolhouse were made by the same boot."

The undertaker gazed at the tracks. He scratched his nose, wrinkled his brow, took hold of his chin whiskers and paced around the tracks. "Something about these strike a chord in my mind. What it is, I can't remember. Maybe I've seen them before."

"Think you know who made this track?"

"Let me work on it a bit. Maybe I can remember what I know about these tracks."

"Try, Jim!" urged Doc. "Soon as you think of something let me know."

Jim nodded. "I'll do that. Let me mull it over."

"O.K., Jim. Why don't you drop by my place for coffee in the morning on your way to work?"

"I'll make it a point."

Jim lurched off down the road heading back towards his

place of business. Doc watched him go and thought about how a man who walked like that should never be off horseback. Jim's retreating figure soon came to the end of Doc's street and turned the corner.

Let him remember, Doc thought. *Let him remember soon! I want this settled.*

Chapter 11

When Doc opened the front door of his house, a powerful odor struck his nostrils. He stopped and sniffed. Pie! Fresh, hot, pecan pie! Doc fished the derringer out of his hip pocket. Someone was in his kitchen. He crossed the living room in three jumps and poked his head and gun through the doorway of the kitchen. There stood Opie ridding up the baking mess. A fresh-baked pie was cooling on top of the table.

"How did you get in here?" demanded Doc, putting up the gun and feeling pretty silly.

"Through the front door." Opie continued washing dishes.

"But how? I thought the door was locked when I left this morning."

Opie put some pans on the drainboard. She looked fresh and cool for a woman who had just finished making a pie. "A mite forgetful, aren't you, pardner? The door was shut, but unlocked. Just dropped in to give you a sample of my culinary art. Found you was out. Decided to make you a pie. They say the way to a man's heart is through his stomach."

Doc felt his neck redden. "Now, Opie, don't start that again this morning! Why aren't you in school?"

"I didn't feel like going today and anyway it happens to be Saturday." She washed a few more dishes. "Sure you don't need a live-in cook?"

"Not just yet." Doc grinned at her. "But I'll keep you in mind."

"I might get a better offer 'most any day now. By the way, did you have you a glass and wall wrecking party last night? I cleaned up a bit of broken windowpane and some shavings from where you whittled your wall. It beats all get out how you wild young bachelors spend your time."

"Somebody took a shot at me last night. They missed. But it kind of rattled me. Hell! It scared me to death."

Opie's blue eyes searched his face. She was plainly disturbed. "I forgot to clean up the mess this morning," Doc added. "If I'd a knowed you was coming, I wouldn't have left the litter."

"That's O.K. Women like to tidy up after the weaker sex. Makes us feel needed and wanted."

Doc remembered something. "Opie, the guy who shot at me last night was the one who listened to our conversation at the schoolhouse. I found his tracks across the street this morning and they matched the prints we found by the school. Jim was with me."

Opie finished the last dish. She dried her long, sure hands on a towel. "And what did you two masterminds come up with?"

"Nothing much," admitted Doc. "The right boot heel was worn down. Jim thinks he might remember who wears out his boots that way."

Opie moved over closer to Doc, surprisingly graceful. "What did Jim want to tell you about Jeanne?"

"That he thinks the gun was in her hand when someone shoved it around as it went off."

Opie made a disappointed face. "That's not much help, is it?"

"Not much. But I've still got two good prospects on my list, Bill and Bob."

Opie gave him a swift look and changed the direction of the conversation. "Doc, you got a horse and buggy?"

"No." Doc wondered what she was up to. "Why?"

"Thought you might like to take a girl for a ride. If you had a horse."

"Where was you hankering to ride to?"

Opie gave an airy wave of her hands. "Oh, the same place all the young bloods take their girls. Maybe the Casa Grande ruins. Shouldn't be anybody else out there on Saturday morning. Wouldn't be nobody within calling range if you decided to

take advantage of the situation and put your arm around me—
or something desperate like that."

Doc knew Opie was joshing him. He also figured that she
probably had something else to say to him and didn't want any
eavesdroppers to hear. He decided to humor her.

"If you're sure I can have my wicked way with you, I'll run
over to the livery barn and rent a trotting rig. Sure you won't
get cold feet and run off the minute I leave here?"

"I won't leave. I'll finish cleaning the house. By the time you
get back with the horse and buggy, I'll be ready to go with
you."

Doc took another sniff of the pie. "How did you know pecan
pie is my favorite?"

Opie dimpled. "I'll never tell. I know lots of other interesting things about you. Remind me to tell you some of them
when we get the time."

Uncanny that she should know about his liking for pecan
pie. Or was it? Just because he'd never paid much attention to
Opie didn't mean she hadn't been studying him for a long
time. That was a sort of warming, flattering thought and he
began to feel eager about their outing. She was fun and whole-
some and made him want to laugh again. Made him feel alive.

He found Bryce sitting in the front office of the stable.
"Hey," Doc greeted his friend. "Where's that horse of a different
color you had for rent?"

"Was you aiming to go joy riding or on serious business?"
queried Bryce.

"It's a joy ride."

Bryce nudged Doc with his elbow. "Who's your gal?"

"Opie."

"You sly old dog, you." Bryce's eyes gleamed with interest.
"Here you been accusing me of being a lady-killer and all the
time you've been plotting to get Opie off to yourself." He
moved over to his desk and looked at a list. "I have just the
right horse for you. A trotter that moves when you want him to
and stands steady as a rock if you get busy when the buggy isn't
moving."

Doc went along with Bryce's kidding. "Guess I might be glad for a trick horse that will either stand or run. How about a buggy?"

"The only one I've got available right now," Bryce looked again at his list, "is over at Bill McClure's forge being repaired. Why don't you go on home and I'll pick up the buggy and deliver it in about half an hour? Bill should have it fixed by then."

"O.K., but hurry it up. Opie's over at my house right now cleaning it up and she'll get it so clean I'll be downright uncomfortable."

Bryce's melodious laugh filled the office. "Never fear. I'll rescue you. Just tell Opie the cavalry is on its way."

When Doc got back to his house, he found Opie had finished cleaning the kitchen and was sitting in his favorite chair in the front room. He shuffled over to the overstuffed settee and gingerly sat down. It was a woman-sized piece of furniture and Doc's long legs propped his knees up in an awkward position in front of him.

"What's the matter, high pockets? Have I got your chair?"

"It doesn't matter, Opie. Sit where you like."

"It does too matter." She got up and took another chair. "A man's got exclusive rights to his own chair."

Doc chuckled and moved over to his own chair. "Opie, how come you keep on kidding me?"

Opie moved over to the settee that faced Doc's chair. "I'm not kidding. Never been more serious in my whole life."

Doc decided to level with this delightful woman. He felt she deserved complete honesty. "Opie, I'm fifty years old. I'm getting soft and out of shape. I haven't gotten over Jeanne yet—and I'm not sure I ever will. I'm set in my ways. It would be hard for a woman to live with me. I don't know if I'm even capable of ever loving anyone again."

Opie gave Doc a steady, valiant smile. "That's a chance I'm willing to take. In time I could make you forget a lot of things that have happened. I already made you forget that horse and buggy you supposedly went after. You did remember to go to the livery stable, didn't you?"

"Bryce didn't have a rig ready right then. The only one available was at the forge getting some repairs. He said he'd bring it around pretty soon. Are you that anxious to get me off alone?"

"You bet your boots, sonny, and I need a private place. Can't think of a more deserted spot than the ruins." She looked out the window. "There's Bryce with the horse and buggy now."

They rose and went out the front door. Bryce stepped down from the buggy and waited at the front gate.

"Well, well, well!" he intoned. "Does my heart good to see a woman coming out of Doc's house again. You been in there very long, Opie?"

"Not long enough." Opie gave Bryce an amused glance as he handed her up into the buggy.

Bryce grinned and patted Doc on the arm. "Don't forget what I told you about this horse. He'll do whatever you want him to."

"I'll put him through his paces." Doc cracked the whip and they pulled away.

It was only about ten miles from Gila Crossing to the Casa Grande ruins. The trotter Bryce had rented to Doc could do a mile in less than three minutes. That is, he could have if Doc had wanted to race him. However, for a ten-mile pull it was best to let the horse set his own pace.

In the fall of the year the Arizona desert country presented a monotonous view of sand, sage brush, and saguaro cactus. The worst of the summer heat was over, but it was still hot enough to fry eggs on the sun-soaked rocks. Riding in a buggy with a top, pulled along smartly by a good horse, the heat wasn't too oppressive.

"You drive pretty good for a man who hasn't done it for three years. Did they let you go joy riding at Yuma?"

"Not so you'd notice." Doc grimaced. "I got me a ride going over and one coming back. And that was the extent of my gallivanting for three years."

"After you finally ask me the fatal question, we'll have to get us a surrey with a fringe on the top. Then you can take me driving every Sunday. People will be envious when they see what a handsome couple we make behind our matched team of grays."

"Don't believe I'd care for grays." Doc pulled at the reins to negotiate a turn in the road.

"Then you have thought about asking me to marry you?"

"How did you get an idea like that, woman?" Then Doc realized she was pulling his leg again. "Come on, Opie. Please talk sensible for a change. What's on your mind that needs so much privacy?"

Opie searched for words. "It's not that I need privacy so much as that I couldn't tell you this in Jeanne's house. This is going to shock you. I might as well get it over with." Opie bit her lip and gazed at him pleadingly. "Doc, the consensus of the gossip line is that Jeanne had a boyfriend before you came along. A serious one. Nobody can say who he was, but nearly everyone thinks she had a fellow. Women can tell when another woman's being courted."

Doc felt a stab of jealousy, fought it down. At this late date he shouldn't feel this way. But he did. Jeanne had been true to him, he was sure. Their union had been complete. And yet— the news of a previous love caused Doc pain.

"Well," he said after a moment, "I'm not surprised. How could I blame a man for falling in love with Jeanne? She must have broken it off when we were married. If she had a boyfriend and he was mad about her marrying me instead of him, that might explain her murder."

Doc eased the horse skillfully down a steep grade. "I've had it in the back of my mind that whoever killed Jeanne was trying to force her to do something. That would explain her having the gun with her the night she was killed. Maybe this former boyfriend was hounding her and she knew they've have a showdown that night. Are you sure none of the women you talked with knew the name of the man?"

"No one knows who it was. Jeanne went around with first

one and then another. But from the way she acted, and some of the things she did, the women figure she was serious about one man." Opie touched his hand. "Don't seem like I ever do you a whole lot of good, do I?"

Doc was very conscious of the touch of Opie's hand on his. A tingling sensation ran through his fingers. "You help me more than you know, Opie."

They had just come up a long rise in the road. As the buggy reached the crest of the rise, the Casa Grande ruins came into view. Doc stopped the horse. He and Opie gazed at the distant ruins. Sun-drenched, the ruins shimmered in the distance, adobe walls taking on a golden patina from reflected sun. Before them the road stretched in a long downgrade that challenged the driver of every horse-drawn rig to a race with himself. Doc was no exception. He accepted the exhilarating prospect of a fast downhill run and whipped up his horse. The buggy plunged over the crest of the hill, accelerating rapidly as horse and gravity pulled the buggy faster and faster down the grade. Halfway down the hill, while the buggy's speed was still increasing, there was a sound like the crack of a high-powered rifle.

The linchpin! That kingpin, upon which the whole front-wheel assembly of the buggy hung and swiveled, had snapped in two! Then, so quickly Doc could only put his arms around Opie and try to protect her with his body, the wheels separated from the buggy, and then the crushing bulk of it tipped downward, hurling its human burden into the dust of the road as it somersaulted over their prostrate forms. Still connected to the shafts and harness, the clattering, bouncing front buggy wheels urged the horse on in a mad race of fear.

The merest chance kept Doc and Opie from being killed. As the broken buggy tipped them out, a big rock caught the front edge of the rig, flipped it in a high bounce so that it narrowly missed crushing them. The buggy rolled over and over many times before coming to rest at the bottom of the hill.

Doc stirred groggily. Opie had landed underneath him. She was scratched and tumbled, but breathing. He disentangled himself. Every bone in his body ached. His practiced hands began to examine Opie. Her eyelids fluttered. Slowly her eyes opened and focused on Doc.

"Hurt any place?" he asked her. "You don't seem to have any broken bones."

"Keep on checking," Opie suggested, sitting up and looking ruefully at her soiled dress. "Say, lover, you sure play rough when you want to get next to a girl. No need to bust the buggy. I'd a given up easy if you had just said what you had in mind."

Doc sighed. "Never stop, do you?"

He pulled Opie to her feet and gently hugged her. They stood there for a moment, her head against his shoulder. Doc was startled at how glad he was she wasn't hurt, also at some other feelings. Settling Opie in the shade of a lonely tree, he went to look at the buggy.

The conveyance was smashed beyond repair. It lay at the bottom of the hill in a forlorn heap of wood and fabric. Doc yelled back at Opie: "Wait there! I'm going to catch the horse."

The horse had run for nearly a mile before coming to a stop in the shade of the Casa Grande ruins. He still had the shafts and the front wheels of the livery rig connected to his harness. Doc went up to the tired horse, but his gaze fastened on the linchpin.

There were smooth, shiny marks on half of the top surface of the remaining portion of the exposed pin. It had been filed almost in two! Someone had weakened it so that it would break under strain. Doc went cold to think of what might have happened if that rock hadn't been just where it was.

Someone had tried to kill him again and hadn't cared if Opie died, too. Doc grew icily furious. The vehicle had been in Big Bill's shop before Bryce delivered it. Doc was sure as hell going to see Bill when he got back to town, give him a big surprise.

"They don't make linchpins very strong these days, do they?" Opie asked from behind him. Her hair was a mess and her clothes were dirty. She looked very beautiful to Doc.

"This one would've lasted longer if someone hadn't cut it

most of the way through." Doc touched the file marks. "I'm going to have this out with Bill McClure when I get back to town." Then he remembered he'd left Opie under the tree. "You should have waited for me. Do you mind riding double?"

"Mind? Best chance I've ever had to get your arms around me."

He shook his head. What a woman. Shaken and bruised from what could have been fatal, she still could joke. And remind him of her intention. Doc took the harness off the horse and led it out of the wheel shafts. Rolling the long rein into shorter lengths, he draped them over the horse's neck, turned, and lifted Opie up onto the horse's back. She was lighter than she looked. Then he climbed on behind her and they rode back towards town.

It was a good feeling to have a woman in his arms again. Opie, as though divining his thoughts, leaned back and rested her head on his shoulder. The warm, woman smell of her; clean, pleasant odor of her hair; soft, melting touch of her body; all these things distracted Doc though he tried to concentrate on how to handle Bill. Even when Bill became a prime suspect, it had been hard to think he really had shot Jeanne; and it was impossible to believe that she'd ever had an affair with him. All the same, there was that filed linchpin.

Doc's nerves tightened. No need to be subtle. He'd get his gun and go calling. But for now, didn't Opie feel just like she fitted his arms?

They rode thus, lightly embraced, the few miles back to town. Doc turned the horse into the main street and headed for the livery stable. From a distance they could see a considerable crowd in front of the undertaker's building. The townspeople were staring at Jim Balinte's display window. An uproar of many voices filled the air. A woman screamed.

Doc urged the trotter onward. When they came to the edge of the crowd, he asked a bystander what was wrong.

"Don't rightly know, Doc. I jist got here. Seems there's a corpse on display in Balinte's fancy coffin."

Doc jumped off the horse leaving Opie holding the reins. He pushed through the dense crowd. When he reached the display window and stared at the gray coffin, his heart turned over.

Jim Balinte lay in the coffin.

Chapter 12

Doc could hardly believe his eyes. Yet it was true. That was Jim stretched out in the gray display model casket.

Doc worked through the people surrounding the window and got to the front door of the undertaking establishment. He took a deep breath and went in. Coming up to the coffin he looked down at his friend. His hand sought for a pulse at the carotid artery. There was none. Sticking out of the left side of Jim's chest was the bloody handle of a knife. Doc automatically reached down to pull it free. Then, remembering another death, he jerked his hand back. He wasn't going to get caught with another death instrument in his hand.

Staring down at Jim, he fought a rising nausea. Why Jim? Had he been too close on the heels of Jeanne's killer? Did Jim know who the killer was? Doc wished futilely that he'd never involved Jim in his search for vengeance. He'd never dreamed his friend would suffer for helping him. But the killer had another debt to pay now. No matter what it took, Doc would see that whoever had done this frightful thing would be paid in full.

The door to the mortuary opened again. Amos Dalton stepped in and came over to stand beside Doc. The sheriff's face hardened. The muscles in his lean jaws worked. Through clenched teeth his voice came with an effort. "What dirty bastard did this?"

Doc shook his head and then related his last conversation with Jim. "He was trying to figure out who'd made some tracks that have been dogging me. Looks like whoever it was wanted to make sure Jim didn't talk."

"Why would Jim's killer put his body here in the display window?" wondered Amos. "It doesn't make sense." The sheriff examined the corpse. "I don't think Jim was killed here," he said straightening up. "There's no blood stains on the inside of the coffin. It looks like the blood on the knife and body was dry before he was put in there. Besides, there's drag marks on the floor. Looks to me like the killer dragged Jim in here and stuck him in the coffin. Who in hell would do such a thing—kind of gloat?"

"Somebody with a sick mind, Amos." Doc's backbone felt chill, but he was too mad to worry much about himself. "We're dealing with someone who's crazy enough to kill more than once."

Amos beckoned a couple of the townsmen to come inside. He carefully closed the lid to the coffin and turned to the two men. "I want you boys to stand guard on this coffin and not let anybody else come in." Amos stuck his head out through the front door. "You folks go on about your business. I'll take care of this."

The crowd murmured assent and slowly started to thin out. Amos turned to Doc. "You track and I'll follow along. Let's start with the drag marks on the floor here."

Doc had already noticed the marks on the floor of the mortuary. Marks made by the heels of Jim's boots as his body had been dragged across the floor. The marks led in from the back door.

Following the tracks, Doc and Amos stepped outside. The drag marks continued on around behind the next door livery stable and led up to the back door of McClure's blacksmith shop. Doc and Amos stood before the closed door. They regarded one another silently. Then, nodding agreement, Amos pulled out his gun and Doc opened the door.

There was no one in the shop. The forge was empty.

"Wonder where Bill is?" Amos looked around the empty room. "I didn't notice him in the crowd at the undertaking parlor. Kind of thought we'd find him here."

"So did I." Doc motioned to a spot on the dirt floor. "See

here! This must be where Jim bought it." He pointed to blood stains in the dirt. "And look at the tracks. Same prints Jim and I found in the vacant lot across from my house. That right heel mark! It's blurred from the heel being worn down."

Amos hunkered down to examine the bootprints. "What's this about the heel being worn?"

"I forgot to tell you, Amos. Someone took a shot at me last night. This morning Jim and I found tracks that match these. Jim thought he had an idea of who made them."

Amos scratched his head. "Looks like the trail ends here. Where's Bill? Maybe he can tell us about these blood stains."

"He needs to explain something else, too," Doc said heavily. "Somebody filed down the linchpin of the buggy I was just driving today. The rig came out of Bill's shop shortly before I got it. When the pin broke it upset the buggy and damn near killed me and Opie."

"The hell it did!" choked Amos just as his deputy stuck his head through the front door of the forge. "Sid, you seen Big Bill?"

"I saw him hightailing it out of town about an hour ago, Sheriff. I yelled at him as he went by and asked him what his hurry was. He just kept on riding."

"Wish you'd stopped him," Amos growled. "He needs to tell us a few things. We better go after him. You coming, Doc?"

"You kidding?"

Bryce's night man quickly got Amos and Sid their regular mounts and fetched a rental horse for Doc. They headed out of town towards the Gila River. At the riverbank they cut for sign.

"What kind of horse was Bill riding?" Amos questioned Sid.

"His big bay mare." Sid pointed to a set of tracks that ran south along the riverbank. "Her feet are bigger than most of the cow ponies' around here. Shouldn't be too hard to follow her tracks."

"You cross the river and look for a trail on the other bank, Sid," Amos ordered. "We'll follow along this side. Give a yell if you spot where he crossed."

Sid put his horse to the ford. Amos and Doc followed the tracks.

"Where's he headed?" Amos puzzled as he scanned the trail. "He should have crossed the river back there if he was going to stay with the usual road."

"Looks like he's hightailing it for Tucson." Doc swung his horse into an easy lope alongside Amos. "It don't look like he was planning on going back to Gila Crossing." Doc kicked his horse into a gallop. "Let's try our damnedest to catch him, Amos."

"We might catch him," Amos allowed, spurring his mount. "He's only got an hour's head start."

Sid gave a resounding shout from the other bank. Amos and Doc reined in their horses. The river was only about one hundred feet wide at that point. The bank Doc and Amos were on was considerably higher than the other side of the river. They were silhouetted against the sky as they looked across to where Sid had called from among a small clump of trees.

"What is it, Sid?" yelled Amos.

"Better come over here, Sheriff."

Amos and Doc splashed their horses across the shallow river. Sid was off his horse examining the ground before him in a small clump of trees. He pointed to an empty cartridge case in the sand at the base of one tree. "Looks like somebody set up an ambush on this side of the river and fired at something on the other side."

Amos and Doc took in the signs that said a lone man had hunkered down among the trees and waited. They saw the butt ends of a couple of hand-rolled cigarettes, several burnt wooden matches, and marks where the assassin had laid his rifle down while waiting for his shot.

And finally, there was the brass shell case. Amos picked up the piece of brass and sniffed at it. "Still fairly fresh smoke smell. It's a .30 caliber rimfire. Must've been fired in the last hour. Anything else on this side, Sid?"

"Only the gunman's tracks going back into the brush the

same way he came out." Sid pointed off towards the higher ground.

"You go take a look at where them tracks go, Sid. We'll cross back over and keep after Bill. May have to go on to Tucson. After you follow your trail for a while, double back to town and tell my wife where I went. Also ask around and see if you can find out what Bill was up to when he left town."

"O.K., Amos." Sid mounted his horse. "See you when you get back."

Amos and Doc cut back across the river and saw where Bill's horse had reared, probably when the ambusher had fired, and then raced on. The two men resumed their tracking.

About three hundred yards down the trail they found Big Bill. He was laying in the mud by a small clump of brush. His horse had disappeared. Bill had been shot through the back just under his left shoulder. He still breathed.

It was a tribute to Bill's monumental strength that he'd been able to ride for nine hundred feet before the shock of the wound had caused him to fall.

Doc jumped down from his horse and quickly staunched the flow of blood from Bill's back wound with a handkerchief.

"Got another piece of cloth on you, Amos? I need to plug up his front, too."

Amos volunteered his neckerchief and helped Doc turn the giant over. The bullet had passed clear through Bill's body and exited near the collarbone. The angle at which the bullet had struck pointed upward. If it had been a few inches lower, it would have passed through his heart. As it was, he was still in bad shape.

Bill's clothing was muddy from where he had plowed into the river bottom. He had lost one boot when he fell from the saddle. Blood stained his shirt, front and back, and his face had a ghastly pallor. He looked more dead than alive.

The two men hurriedly cut a couple of saplings from the riverbank and made a rude travois to carry the wounded man. Big Bill was too heavy for them to lift up onto a horse, even if he hadn't been too badly wounded to stand the jogging. Straining, they rolled Bill onto the improvised carrier and lashed it to Doc's horse. Then they turned their horses back towards town.

When they turned into the main street of Gila Crossing, people flowed out of stores and houses and followed them to Doc's house. Several men helped them carry the fallen giant into Doc's medical examination room.

Doc reached for his medical kit. Someone was sent off to fetch Bill's wife, Heather. Then Amos made the crowd of people move outside the house. Doc got his surgical tools and went to work on Bill's wounds, patched them as best he could, and was just finishing when Heather ran into the room.

Heather was a statuesque young woman. Her massive dignity was a match to the man she had married. She carried herself well. Her shining black hair topped off her ample figure in a manner that caused people to turn and stare. She and her blacksmith husband made an impressive pair.

Heather fell on her knees beside the bunk and put her hand to Bill's cheek. "Where'd it happen?"

"Someone bushwhacked him down along the river," said Amos. "Heather, do you know why he was heading for Tucson?"

Her voice shook and she closed her eyes. "He came by and said someone had sent for him and that he'd be back soon." She stared from Doc to Amos. "Why would anyone want to shoot my Bill?"

Amos sighed. "Heather, it looks like Bill might have had something to do with Jim being killed."

Heather swung towards Bill as if to shield him from them. Bright spots burned in her cheeks and her straightforward gaze was disconcerting. "My Bill's the most gentle man alive! He never killed anyone! You—you're crazy!" She flung herself into a chair and sobbed as though her heart were broken.

The men watched helplessly. Finally Doc went to Heather and gently touched her shoulder. He pulled a small towel out of a drawer and handed it to her so she could dry her tears.

"I'm sorry, Heather," he said gruffly. "We don't know what else to think. Amos and I followed the tracks that led from

Jim's body to Bill's forge. There was blood on the floor by the anvil. It looks like that's where Jim was killed. Sid told us he'd seen Bill lighting a shuck out of town. We followed his trail. When it came to the river, he'd turned and was heading towards Tucson when we found him." Doc hesitated, hating to hurt her, but not knowing what else to do. "It sure looks to me like he was running away."

Heather blew her nose. "You better look again, Doc. Bill never ran away from anything in his whole life. Running's not his style. If he had done anything wrong he'd have stayed and faced the music."

"Dammit!" Doc looked from Heather to Amos. "I don't know what to think. This whole thing's a nightmare. It seems to me like Jim's death is tied up with Jeanne's. Jim was helping me sort out some clues related to Jeanne's death. Somebody silenced him."

Heather shook her raven tresses. "It wasn't my Bill! Why do you think he—he killed Jim? And what's that got to do with Jeanne?"

"On the night she was killed, five of my best friends were missing from the party at the same time. I've already checked the alibis of everyone except Bill and Bob. Can you tell me where Bill disappeared to that night?"

Heather began to laugh. Fearing she was becoming hysterical, Doc started to shake her but she pushed him away.

"Sure! I know where he was when he left the party." The spectators leaned forward expectantly. "He was out walking in the side yard with me," Heather explained. "It was hot in the house. We were just getting some fresh air. When all the commotion started, we both came running with the rest of the people. He was with me all the time."

Doc's mouth fell open. If what Heather had just told him was true, then Bill couldn't have killed Jeanne. If Bill hadn't killed Jeanne, chances were he hadn't killed Jim. Still, wives have been known to cover up for their husbands. The tracks had led to Bill's forge. He had been heading for Tucson. There just had to be a reason for Bill's actions this night.

"All right, Heather," Doc said cautiously, "but Bill's still got some questions to answer. I've patched him up as good as I can. Now we'll have to wait until he can talk before we find out what he was up to tonight. Why don't you go home and get some rest? There's nothing you can do here."

"You're wrong again, Doc," replied Heather. Her smile was wobbly but determined. "I can help him get well just by staying with him." She rose and moved her chair over to where Bill lay.

Doc turned to Amos. "Let's go over to my kitchen and have a drink."

The two men left Heather sitting by her wounded husband and passed into the other part of the house. Doc found a bottle of whiskey and poured out two large drinks. Amos tossed his shot down and Doc drained his glass in a single gulp. They sat down at the kitchen table.

The two men stared at their empty glasses for a few moments. "Well, Doc, looks like you're down to one last suspect. I didn't notice Bob around when Jim's body was found today. And where was he when Bill was shot? Reckon we better go over to his house and have a talk with him?"

"Not tonight, Amos." Doc's tone of voice brooked no argument. "I don't want to rush into any more fast conclusions like I did with Bill. I need to think everything through tonight. I'll go see Bob first thing in the morning. If he's my man, I want him to have a whole night to think over his sins. Then maybe he'll be ready to talk business by tomorrow."

Amos nodded his agreement. "Just one thing."

"What's that, Amos?"

Amos held out his hand. "Give me your gun."

Doc gave the sheriff a long look. "I don't aim to gun him down." He reached into his hip pocket and took out his derringer. He handed it to Amos. As he did so, there came a knock and then the front door of the house opened. In stepped Opie.

Chapter 13

"I heard about Bill being shot," she said as she closed the door and moved into the room. "Is he hurt bad?"

"Pretty bad," Doc nodded. "But with a little luck he'll pull through."

Amos got to his feet. "I'd better move along. Need some sleep after this long day. I'll see you tomorrow. 'Night, Opie."

Opie sat down in a chair. "Have you found out anything about Bill? Do you think he might have killed Jim?"

"How'd you know he's under suspicion?"

Opie smiled at him. "It's a small town. Jim's body was in the window. You and Amos and Sid left town in a hurry. Bill had gone earlier. The word gets around."

"I don't know much, Opie," said Doc. "Quite a bit of circumstantial evidence seems to point at Bill, but he's unconscious and can't talk yet. Heather has given him an alibi for the night Jeanne was killed. If he's in the clear about Jeanne's death, then it's a good bet he didn't kill Jim. He wouldn't have any reason to otherwise. But then, Heather might not be telling the truth seeing as how she's married to him."

Opie frowned. "I've never known Heather to lie about anything."

"Neither have I," admitted Doc. "At this point I really don't know about Bill. We'll just have to wait until he can talk to find out what he knows about all this."

"Then you're down to just one good suspect—Bob Noel."

Doc studied Opie's face. "Looks like it. I'm sure going to have a talk with him in the morning." Then Doc remembered where he had left Opie when he found Jim's body.

"I'm sorry about running off and leaving you sitting on the horse in the middle of the street." Doc colored. "Didn't think what I was doing."

Opie waved her hand. "Don't fret about it, Doc. You had other things on your mind. I took the horse back to the livery stable and went on home."

"Thanks for being such a good sport about it," Doc stifled a yawn. "Opie, it's getting late. I'm tired. Would you mind . . ."

Opie jumped up. "Oh. I'm sorry. You've had a hard day." She bent over and kissed him on the cheek. "Good night, Doc." The front door fanned a slight breeze as she passed out into the night.

Doc sat there tingling. A long time since a woman had kissed him. It felt good. Opie's brief kiss lingered on his cheek, making him feel like a whole man again. His step was light as he crossed over to his office and looked in on Heather and Bill. Bill still slept. Heather was sitting in a chair beside him.

Doc checked Bill's pulse, listened to his breathing, and examined the bandages. He found nothing amiss with his patient.

"I'm going to turn in, Heather. You're welcome to sleep on the sofa in the front room if you like."

Heather leaned back in her chair. "I couldn't sleep. I'll stay here by Bill."

"Give a yell if you need me." Doc went out the office door and into his front room. He locked the front door of the house and gave a sigh of relief that this day was over.

Was Bob Noel the killer? Hard to believe. Elegant, suave, solid, Bob. But it was a possibility. And who killed Jim?

Poor Jim! Doc felt sick when he confronted the fact that his friend would probably still be alive if he hadn't got mixed up in Doc's quest for vengeance.

Doc took off his clothes and hopped in bed. He tossed and turned for what seemed like hours. When he finally gave up trying to sleep he found that only an hour had passed. He got out of bed, clumped down the stairs, and without bothering to light a lamp, sat down at his kitchen table. Memories swept over him.

He remembered the good times around this very table. His five friends playing poker. Jeanne joking with the men. Jim Balinte being philosophical. Bryce being funny. Amos' flashing fingers deftly dealing cards. Big Bill almost breaking the chair with his weight. Banker Noel playing five-card draw as though the pot money really meant something to him. Things had been simpler then.

And what now? Jim gone along with Jeanne. Bill with a lot of questions to answer when he regained consciousness. Bob Noel sitting over in his big house; safe, secure, for this one last night.

Christ! I hope Noel ain't getting any more sleep than I am. Wish I'd let Amos talk me into seeing Bob tonight. Guess I'll just sit here the rest of the night. Ain't no use going back bed. Couldn't sleep anyhow. And Doc promptly went to sleep sitting up at the kitchen table.

He awoke with a crick in his neck and his head hurting from where it had rested on the hard table. It was morning. He quickly dressed, put the coffee pot on to boil, and then went to check up on his patient. Bill was still in a coma, but his vital signs were good. Doc persuaded Heather to come over to the kitchen for a cup of coffee. She told him she had napped on and off during the night and went back to sit by her husband.

Doc hurried over to Noel's house. He knocked on the front door. Delia came to answer.

"The top of the morning to ye, Doctor. May I ask what brings ye calling at this early hour?"

Doc returned Delia's greeting and moved into the house. "I want to see Mr. Noel. Would you please tell him I'm here?"

"Certainly I will. Would ye be so kind as to step into the office and wait? It will be only a shake till Mr. Noel finishes dressing. I'll be going and tell him ye be waiting."

"Thank you, Delia."

Doc walked down the hallway and entered Noel's office. It was the first time he had been there for over three years. The room was the same as he remembered. There were shelves full of books. Several paintings hung on the walls between the shelves. A large, ornate mirror gleamed over the fireplace. Bob's desk and chair occupied one corner of the room. Another corner held a glass-fronted gun case.

Doc crossed to the gun case. He opened the door. There were several rifles and handguns on display. One of the rifles was a .30 caliber carbine. Doc reached his hand inside and picked it up. He opened the breech and sighted down the barrel.

Dirty! The rifle had recently been fired. He closed the breech and chambered a fresh shell.

"Do you like my gun?" came Bob's voice from behind him.

Doc slowly turned, the gun in his hands. His finger tightened on the trigger. He swung the barrel of the gun until it was pointing at Noel.

Bob looked fresh and dapper. His hair was neatly combed, cheeks freshly shaved, no dark circles of worry showing under his eyes. A faint mocking smile was on his lips. Doc held the rifle steady and looked at Bob. Noel stared steadily back at him.

So easy to pull the trigger! A moment of blind fury and one man would be dead. And the other? Wouldn't he kill something in himself at the same moment? It was one thing to think about killing a man, another thing to do it. Besides, Noel might not be the one. Doc lowered the gun barrel, replaced the carbine in the case, and closed the door.

Noel walked over and sat down at his desk. He motioned for Doc to take a chair facing him, reached into a humidor and pulled out a fresh cigar, and indicated Doc was to help himself. Doc refused. Noel bit the end off his stogie and struck a match. In a moment he had the cigar going. He blew out a thin stream of smoke.

"That was close."

"You'll never know how close, Bob. I wanted to kill you— but I couldn't."

"I'm glad you didn't pull the trigger, Doc, because I didn't kill Jeanne. And I didn't kill Jim either."

"How did you know that's what I've been thinking?" asked Doc.

"Not much goes on in my town that I don't know about. You've been asking a lot of questions, talking to a lot of people. Most of your conversation got back to me shortly after you spoke the words. I know you've been checking out the alibis of your five best friends."

"Nice, tight little organization you've got in this town," Doc grunted.

The banker drew on his cigar and blew a smoke ring. "A man in my position has to know what's going on. A lot depends upon my knowledge of affairs in this town. I have to make decisions every day based on what I know. Information is my stock in trade."

"All right, Bob. If you know so damned much, tell me something."

"What do you want to know?"

"Where were you when Jeanne was killed? You'd left the ballroom. I don't know where you went."

Noel considered the ash on the end of his cigar. "I was here in this office talking to a business associate. A man by the name of David Burns, a banker from Show Low, came in on the evening stage that night. We had some pressing business. He came to the house and called me away from the party. We stepped into my office for a few moments. I was talking to him when the commotion started."

"I hope you can get him to back up your story."

"Oh, I can. It just so happens that Dave's coming to see me at the bank today. You can see him if you wish."

Too easy. Too smooth. "Where were you last night when Jim's body was found?" Doc demanded. "And a little later when Amos and I found a .30 caliber shell on the riverbank right across from where someone had shot Bill?"

"Out west of town. Target practicing in the sandpit."

"I suppose you can produce a witness for that story too?" jabbed Doc.

"Yes. Someone was with me last evening." Bob turned and

pulled on a bell cord that hung on the wall. Presently Delia answered.

"Delia," said Bob, "would you please ask my wife to come here."

"Certainly, Mr. Noel." Delia curtsied.

In a few moments Bob's wife entered. Ruth Noel was a true product of the Old South. Patrician by birth, she carried herself with the air of a great beauty. Deep brown, almost black hair; starlit eyes, even in daytime; small, finely boned body; beauty of face that caused men to gasp; all wrapped up in one lovely delicate woman. Doc always felt a bit of envy for Bob Noel when he was in the presence of Ruth's loveliness and vibrant personality.

"Hello, Doc," she said in a sweetly gracious tone.

"Hello, Ruth."

"Ruth," Noel said to his wife. "Where were you last evening?"

"Why, I was with you."

"Yes, dear. But where were we?"

Ruth looked at her husband as though he had taken leave of his senses. "Robert Noel! Is this some kind of joke? You know perfectly well that we were out at the sandpit shooting your carbine. What's going on here anyway? Why haven't you offered Doc some breakfast? Sometimes, Robert, you act as though you're losing your mind. What's this all about?"

"It just so happens, wife, that Doc is here on a very serious business call and not for pleasure. He wanted to know where I was last night and you've just verified what I told him. Now, if you will excuse us, we have some unfinished business to talk over."

"Well! I certainly don't want to intrude! Good day, Doctor!" Ruth swept out of the room.

Bob gave Doc a crooked grin. "You can bet I'll catch hell about that dismissal later. Is there anything else I can tell you?"

"No. That pretty well accounts for you at the moment." Doc wasn't ready to give up completely on Noel. "If you don't mind, I'll go along to the bank and talk to Dave Burns." *Not*

that you couldn't bribe him to lie. You have everyone else in
your pocket. And did you ever have Jeanne in your arms?

"Go right ahead, Doc. Tell you what. I'll stay home until
you've had a chance to talk to Dave. When you see him, tell
him that I'll be along a little later."

"All right, Bob. I'll do that." Doc nodded and left the Noel
house.

On the way to the bank Doc thought about Noel's alibi.
Noel's wife had backed him up on his whereabouts when Jim's
body was found. If the banker, Dave Burns, supported Noel's
story about where he had been on the night Jeanne was killed,
then Doc was at a dead end, though it was possible Burns
might lie.

Of the five men Doc had suspected, all had stories that
checked out. All except Big Bill. Only half of Bill's story was
confirmed. As soon as the giant recovered consciousness, Doc
would question him about where he'd been headed when he
got bushwhacked.

The bank was one of the larger store buildings on the main
street. There was a large plate glass window on the left, an artis-
tically carved door in the center, and another large plate glass
window on the right.

The bank front was a tribute to the success that Bob Noel
had made in the banking business on the frontier. The plate
glass windows alone had cost a small fortune, not for glass, but
in shipping costs to have them freighted clear across country to
Arizona Territory from Ohio. There were probably no larger
pieces of glass to be found anywhere in the territory. Most large
windows at that time were made up of many small panes of
glass. These were single pieces.

Kept clean and polished daily, the bank's front windows
reflected the bright desert sun like mirrors. Across the face of
each window, in large gilt-edged letters, was Gila Crossing
State Bank. Underneath in smaller, neat letters ran the legend:
Bob Noel, President.

Doc mounted the steps and entered the bank. He crossed the
lobby and addressed himself to the teller on duty. The teller

was a middle-aged man of medium height who had grown rather heavy in his confining line of work. The man looked up and squinted at Doc as he came up to the wicket.

"Dorman," said Doc, "I'm looking for a man by the name of Dave Burns."

"He's waiting in Mr. Noel's office." The teller pointed with his pen towards the office door. "Mr. Noel hasn't come in yet. You may talk to Mr. Burns in the office if you wish."

"Thanks, Dorman." Doc hesitated. "Would you mind telling me who Dave Burns is?"

The teller's speech was clipped and precise just like the figures he was inscribing in the ledger. "He's a banking associate of Mr. Noel. Mr. Burns runs the bank at Show Low. He and Mr. Noel are also partners in several endeavors. Mr. Burns comes to town quite often to see Mr. Noel."

"Does he ever come to town on the late stage and stay overnight?"

"Quite often." Dorman dipped his pen in the inkwell. "Mr. Burns doesn't come around on any regular schedule, just at whatever time he has business with Mr. Noel."

Noel seemed to have been telling the truth about banker Burns. Doc went into Noel's private office.

Dave Burns turned out to be a pleasant-looking man. He was fairly short, stockily built, and had an infectious grin that made Doc like him on sight.

"Hello," said Doc extending his hand. "I'm Killian. I understand that you're Dave Burns."

The other man shook Doc's hand. "You understood right, Killian. I'm Burns. What can I do for you?"

"I've just come from talking with Bob Noel. He told me to tell you he'd be along pretty soon. He also said I could ask you a few questions."

"Ask away. If Mr. Noel sent you, I may tell you more than you'll care to know."

They both sat down and Doc plunged.

"About three years ago, along in the spring of the year, I was at a party at Noel's house. My wife was murdered that night."

"You're *that* Killian," the banker's eyebrows shot up. "Yes, I remember very well the events of that night."

"At the time my wife was killed, Noel said he was in his home office talking to you. Was he?"

"Yes. He was."

Doc had come full circle. With those three simple words the banker had backed up Noel's story, and Burns didn't act like a liar.

If Bill had an excuse, then what? There *was* a killer, still at work. He had to be caught. But how?

"Are you all right, Killian?" The banker looked concerned. "I'm sorry my answer seems to come as a shock."

"It's a shock all right." Doc shook his head wearily. "And a dead end. The men I thought might have killed my wife have all been able to establish alibis. I don't know where to look now."

"I wish I could help you, Killian. But I've told you all I know."

The door to the office opened and Bob Noel came in.

"Hello, Dave." He shook hands with his visitor. "I see you've met Doc."

Dave got to his feet. "Yes, Mr. Noel, we've talked a bit. Afraid I wasn't much help. I'll wait outside." He nodded to Doc and went out the door.

Noel turned to Doc. "Are you satisfied?"

"Yes, Bob." Doc was still reserving judgment, but he didn't want Noel to know that. "Your friend here backs up your story."

Noel's face broke out into a big smile. "I told you I had nothing to hide."

"That's what they all say." Doc grimaced. "All five of you have perfect alibis about what you were doing the night Jeanne was killed."

Noel sat down at his desk. "Doc, has it ever occurred to you that some perfect stranger might have killed Jeanne? A drifter who just happened to be going through that night? Maybe he was attracted to my house by the lights and the noise. He could have been standinig out in the garden playing Peeping Tom when he saw Jeanne alone in the library. What if he took a notion to rob her? He could have gone through the french doors and taken her by surprise."

"Jeanne didn't have her purse."

Noel wasn't used to being interrupted. Frowning, he continued. "The killer wouldn't have known that just from looking through the window. By the time he found out his mistake, Jeanne may have pulled a gun on him. He probably tried to take it away from her and in the struggle Jeanne got shot."

"How did you know about the gun?" Doc asked with quick suspicion. "I thought only Jim and me knew about how Jeanne got killed."

"Like I told you before"—Bob smiled patiently—"information's my stock in trade. I talked to Jim the morning of the day he died. He told me about the mark on Jeanne's finger and what you guys had figured out. Doesn't my theory hold water?"

"It's a possibility." Doc shrugged. "But not much of one. A drifter wouldn't come back now and kill Jim."

"Jim may have died for some completely different reason." Bob's voice was forceful. "I think I've given you the answer to this case. Can't you reconcile yourself to the fact that you may never know who killed Jeanne? Why not admit to yourself that none of us did it and that the person who did will never be found?"

Retorts flocked to Doc's lips, but he held them back. Apart from Jim, there was that shot through the window, the filed linchpin. The killer was no casual long-gone vagrant. He was right here in this town—and he might be the handsome, self-assured man Doc faced now.

"But where does that leave me?" Doc deliberately let self-pity tinge his voice. "I've lost my wife. Three miserable years of my life were spent locked up at Yuma. I can't give up on avenging Jeanne's death."

"What you mean is"—Bob's words were sharp and spaced out—"you can't give up on your own revenge."

"What's the difference?"

Noel set out to lecture Doc as though he were talking to a bank loan defaulter. "Plenty. Revenge is selfish, a personal vendetta that you wage in an effort to get the world to pay you back for your injuries. Revenge has nothing to do with avenging Jeanne's death."

If Bob was the killer, he was also a wonderfully smooth hypocrite. Well, Doc could do some faking, too, pretend to fall for Bob's homily.

"I've never thought of it that way," he said meekly.

Noel's voice and manner softened. "Then you better start thinking a little different than you have since you got back to town. Keep on like you been doing and you're going to be running out of friends."

Or they'll be killed, like Jim. Doc stared at the banker, trying to guess what he really was.

"We're going to bury Jim this afternoon," Bob went on. "I've made the arrangements, except for the eulogy. Would you like to say a few words at the graveside?"

"Yes, I would. He was a special friend of mine. I'd be proud to speak at his funeral."

"Good. The funeral's at two o'clock."

"See you then," said Doc. On his way out, he met Burns and thanked him again, nodded to the teller behind the counter, and went out the front door. Amos Dalton was leaning against the railing in front of the bank.

"Hello, Amos." Doc hadn't expected to see the sheriff. "What are you doing here?"

"Waiting for you to finish your conference."

Doc grinned. "Seems like everyone in this town knows what I'm doing except me."

"That's the way it is." Amos was in no mood to joke. "Doc, you know how we figured Jim got killed next to the anvil in Bill's shop? In our hurry to get after Bill we didn't spend much time looking around. I went back to the forge this morning and found something."

"What?" demanded Doc, heart speeding.

"Jim evidently didn't die right away. He must have lived for a while after he got stuck with that knife. At least he lived long enough to leave you a message."

Doc's pulse hammered. Was this the break he needed? What kind of message?

"It was written on the base of the anvil—in blood."

Chapter 14

Doc and Amos hurried down the street to the blacksmith shop. There were no windows in the front wall, only two doors, large enough to admit a team and wagon. Most of the time they were open because the heat from the fire in the forge made it too hot. Since Big Bill was laid up, the doors were closed and the forge was cold.

Inside, the smithy was mostly open space. Small windows ran along both sides of the building. Hitching rings were stapled at strategic points along the walls. There was one back door. In one of the back corners was a great forge and anvil. The forge was a raised brick hearth, table height, lined with firebrick, on which nestled a bed of coals. A metal hood rose above the coals to connect with a brick chimney. A large bellows at the base of the hearth provided draft for the fire. An ingenious arrangement of ropes, levers, and pulleys let the blacksmith pump the bellows with one foot while he thrust pieces of metal into the heating fire. On each side of the hearth were benches covered with smithy tools.

The anvil, a massive piece of iron, rested on a roughly squared former tree trunk. It stood out a little ways from the forge. The wooden base was worn smooth with years of use. This is where Jim had left his last message.

Doc and Amos knelt to scrutinize the bloody scrawl on the backside of the anvil base.

"Jim must have managed to crawl around and write on the back of the anvil base," said Amos. "That's why we didn't notice the message when we found the body. It must have taken a lot of willpower for him to write this and then crawl back around to the front of the anvil. He wanted to make sure that only you got the word, that the killer didn't see it."

Doc looked at the message. "But why didn't he just write the killer's name?"

"I figure he didn't see who put the knife in him." Amos shifted his weight. "A knife makes an ugly wound. The shock of the knife thrust would probably have made Jim pass out almost immediately. It's my guess that the killer came up behind him, grabbed him around the neck with his left arm, reached over Jim's right shoulder, and slammed the knife into his upper left chest straight towards the heart. That way Jim wouldn't have a chance to see the face of the killer and be able to identify him. Makes me think the killer was somebody Jim knew. If it was a stranger who did it, then he probably would have just knifed Jim in the back, not caring if Jim might turn and see his face."

Doc shuddered. "If Jim passed out when the killer hit him, how could he write the message?"

"Jim probably came to in a minute or two, realized he was dying, and made a last effort to tell you what he knew." Amos stood up. "A puzzling thing about this message is how Jim was able to make it. Evidently when he came to, the killer had gone away for a while and left him alone. After Jim had written the message, the killer must have come back and dragged his body over to the mortuary." Amos took his hat off and ran his hand through his thinning hair. "Don't make too much sense, but that's the way I read it. What do you make of the message?"

Doc studied the scrawl. It was one continuous word. Scribbled in blunt, ragged letters by a dying man with a bloody forefinger. It was hard to decipher. The letters straggled drunkenly across the wooden surface.

The image of his dying friend, in an agony of pain, flashed through Doc's mind. The effort it took to make these letters was almost beyond comprehension. And yet they had been shaped. Made to give Doc some hint to the killer's name. Doc had to blink his eyes to clear them of tears.

Doc read and reread the blood-tinged message. Finally he

was satisfied that he'd read them correctly. They formed three
words strung together with the blood of his friend. Unfortu-
nately the second word was smeared so badly that it was completely illegible. The first word was "think" and the third was
"track."

"I don't guess I can make any more out of the message than
you can, Amos. There's three words here. The first one is
'think' and the third's 'track,' but the second's too blurred to
read. Doesn't make sense without the second word."

"Maybe not." Amos sighed. "Jim was trying to tell you something. It must have been mighty important. Don't the words
strike any kind of echo with you?"

Doc came up out of his squatting position. He was wracking
his brain to try and figure out what the second smeared word
could be. Nothing came. " 'Track' must mean the set of bootprints he and I found the morning after someone took a shot at
me. Maybe the blurred word is someone's name. Jim may not
have seen who stuck the knife in him, but he must have come
up with a good notion as to who had made the tracks."

"Think about it," Amos urged. "Something may come to
you. Meantime I better just cover this message so nobody but
you and me will know it was left."

Amos ran his finger tips along the inside edge of the forge
chimney hood, brought out his hand with fingers covered with
soot and smeared it across the bloody message until no trace
remained.

Doc frowned. "Amos, when Jim and I found the tracks of
my bushwhacker, he kind of acted like he thought he knew
who had made them. He wouldn't say who he thought it was.
Said he wanted to think about it. Even to help me out in my
search he didn't want to take the chance of accusing an innocent person. Evidently he did know who made the tracks. I just
wish I was smart enough to figure out what his first word
means and what the second word is."

Amos dropped his hand on Doc's shoulder. "Don't give up.
Whatever Jim meant, he knew that you'd eventually figure it
out. It'll come to you. Just give it time."

Time? While the killer's on the loose, maybe ready to strike again?

"I'll try," said Doc, but he felt ragingly helpless.

The sheriff started for the front door of the blacksmith shop. "Don't guess we can do any more here right now. We better go home and get cleaned up for the funeral." He closed the doors and locked them. "You want me to stay with you until time to go to the cemetery?"

"No," Doc said grimly. "I almost wish that sneaky bastard who's behind all this would have another try at me. Maybe that's the only way I'll get him."

"If he doesn't get you first."

"If," agreed Doc.

"O.K.," shrugged Amos. "See you at the grave."

The two men went their separate ways.

When Doc got to his house, he sat down in his favorite chair and let his mind drift back to when he had first met Jim Balinte. It was in the first few months of his coming to Gila Crossing.

Doc had been called to treat a patient who was dying, a nine-year-old girl who'd been bitten by a rattlesnake while playing out on the desert. By the time the terrified child had run back to the ranch house, it was too late.

Her parents had loaded her in a wagon and drove as fast as they could the ten miles to town and the doctor. By the time Doc saw the girl, she was in a deep coma and sinking fast. He could do nothing for her.

Doc's helplessness in the face of the child's impending death hit him in a weak moment and almost overwhelmed him. As it had done innumerable times on the battlefields during the war, Doc's sense of the futility of his calling tormented him. His training and experience as a medical man seemed as nothing. Life, or the fact of death, had defeated him again.

When the girl finally died, Doc did a very human thing. He proceeded to get drunk. Sat and drank by himself until he passed into oblivion. This was something he'd never done before.

Sometime during the night Jim Balinte came to get the child's body. He did his work as undertaker and then returned to take care of Doc. He got him to bed, then sat up the rest of the night to be there when Doc woke up.

When Doc opened his eyes the next morning, he saw a strange man sitting at his bedside. "Who are you?" he asked, stifling a groan and blinking.

"Name's Jim Balinte. I'm the undertaker."

Doc shakily swung his legs over the side of the bed. "Haven't seen you around since I've been in town. Heard about you. Been meaning to look you up."

"I should have come to see you, Doctor," Jim said apologetically. "I don't get out much anymore. Aside from attending to my business I hole up with my books most of the time. Sometimes the real world seems a little too much for me to cope with."

"I've been kind of feeling that way myself," admitted Doc.

"Yes, I know. You talked quite a bit in your sleep. I gather that you're disturbed about your calling as a physician, feel like chucking it."

Doc stumbled over to the washstand and splashed cold water on his face. "Right at the moment I sure feel like finding some other line of work. I don't want to watch nine-year-old children dying and not be able to do a thing."

Jim found a towel and put it in Doc's fumbling hands. "That child's death wasn't your fault, Doctor."

"That's easy enough to say." Doc dried his hands and face. "But it doesn't make it any easier to bear."

Jim Balinte rose from his chair. "Come with me," he said.

Reluctantly, wondering if the undertaker was some kind of friendly nut, Doc pulled on his boots and followed Jim out of the house. Jim led him down the street, out to the edge of town, and up to the cemetery. There, among the rough headstones and rude wooden crosses, Jim paused and motioned for Doc to look around.

There wasn't much to see. Just graves. Bare Arizona desert

that had been pushed back a little bit with a white wooden picket fence. A typical graveyard. More barren than most.

"This is my bailiwick," said Jim. "Just as your domain is life, so mine is death. I've buried a good number of the people who rest here. Before I came here there was no regular undertaker in Gila Crossing. When people died their kin or friends buried them in this plot of ground."

Jim placed a plump hand on a grave marker. "As you can see from the tombstones, many people died before my time and many have died since. Who's to say my services are essential? I have no control over death. It doesn't matter whether I'm here or not. People go right on dying. Yet, now that I'm here, I do what I can for my fellow man."

"What's all this got to do with me?" growled Doc. "I'm a trained physician! Supposedly I know something about keeping people alive. I don't seem to be doing a very good job lately."

"The point I'm making, Doctor, is simply this. A man does what he can. Nothing more. Nothing less. Some higher destiny shapes the lives and deaths of people. No mere man, no matter how well trained in the healing arts, can change that. Before you came to town a lot of people died without any medical aid at all. The death rate has dropped considerably since you've been around. People are walking around alive today because of you. Don't sell yourself short. You're really one hell of a doctor."

That was a turning point in Doc's life. Jim had renewed his faith in himself and enabled him to go on in his chosen profession. It was a unique gift. And as Doc got to know Jim better he found out that other people in Gila Crossing were indebted to Jim for similar graces. Now Jim was dead and Doc had to speak at his funeral. *And I'll get whoever killed you, Jim,* Doc vowed. *I swear to do that if I live.*

Soon it was time to go to the cemetery. Doc got up from his chair, washed and combed his hair, changed clothes. The tiny things one did even when a friend was dead. Doc opted to wear his light, party suit. Jim hadn't been a somber man, despite his calling. He'd loved life, and good times, parties, and people.

Jim wouldn't want him to attend his funeral dressed in mourning.

There came a knock on Doc's front door. He went to open it, tense, though he didn't expect the killer to knock. There stood Opie. She was dressed in a flowing, simple white dress embroidered with gay-colored flowers, a dress Jim would have loved. In her hand she held a bouquet of wild flowers.

"Ready to go?" she asked.

Doc offered her his arm and they started the long walk down the street to the cemetery.

Doc was pleased with Opie's appearance. "I'm glad to see we seem to agree on funeral clothes."

"I think this is the way Jim would have liked for us to dress." Opie's eyes filled with tears and her hand tightened on Doc's arm. "He always had an eye for pretty dresses. And—and, bless him, he always made me feel like I was beautiful."

"You are beautiful, Opie."

"Thank you." Opie looked at him doubtfully. "You really mean that?" For Opie was a woman who wouldn't have heard that often, so often that she accepted it as her due.

"I really mean that." Opie's wistfulness got to Doc more than her bantering assaults ever had.

Other people joined them as they drew near the cemetery. Everyone in town was going to be there. Jim had many friends. He was a well-loved man. Yet, someone—possibly an ostensible mourner mingled in with the real ones—had brutally killed him.

When Doc and Opie got to the cemetery, a crowd of several hundred people was gathered at the grave. Men, women, and children stood in a silent semicircle. Jim's hearse was drawn up by the open grave. The ornate gray coffin that had been his display piece rested on the bare earth beside the newly dug grave. Six pallbearers stood by the closed coffin.

"Dearly beloved," the preacher began, "we are gathered here in the sight of God and man to pay our last respects to our departed brother, Jim Balinte. I take my remarks today from the fourteenth chapter of John: 'Let not your heart be troubled: ye believe in God, believe also in me. In my Father's house are many mansions: if it were not so, I would have told you. I go to prepare a place for you. And if I go and prepare a place for you, I will come again, and receive you unto myself; that where I am, there ye may be also. And whither I go ye know, and the way ye know. I will not leave you comfortless: I will come to you. Yet a little while, and the world seeth me no more; but ye see me: because I live, ye shall live also. Peace I leave with you, my peace I give unto you: not as the world giveth, give I unto you. Let not your heart be troubled, neither let it be afraid.' Come Brethren, let us pray."

The assembled people bowed their heads. All around them the limitless sky of the desert absorbed the words of the minister as he recited the Twenty-third Psalm.

"The Lord is my shepherd; I shall not want. He maketh me to lie down in green pastures—" Not a person in the funeral crowd moved. No sound but the melodious voice of the preacher. Even the dogs sat still and silent. "—and I will dwell in the house of the Lord forever. Amen."

"Amen," repeated the people.

The reverend made room for Doc by the coffin. "I should like to call upon brother Killian to say a few words."

Doc stepped up to the coffin and laid one hand upon its top. He paused for a moment and then turned to the crowd. "Jim Balinte wasn't a religious man. Not in the sense of owing allegiance to any one church or creed. I'm not even sure he believed in God. Not, at least, in a wrathful, vengeance-seeking Jehovah who'd punish a man because he didn't belong to any one particular Christian sect."

Doc's words plainly disturbed his audience. They weren't used to thinking a man could be a good Christian without belonging to some church. Doc didn't care. A good time to tempt them to start thinking, maybe.

"Jim's concept of God was a universal force in the universe that desired the brotherhood and evolvement of man. Jim was a free thinker. He never cared what church a man belonged to. Jim only tried to learn each man's needs and fill them if he could. Jim's greatest gift was that he could sense when a fellow human being was troubled. By his very presence and understanding he helped many of us overcome our troubles."

Doc looked directly at Opie. Her eyes shone and he knew she understood. "Jim helped me once to know I was not alone. His words of comfort gave me a reason for continuing in my work. I shall miss him—forever. His life was a blessing to us all."

The pallbearers lifted the coffin and placed it on boards over the open grave. Other men held the ends of the ropes that would lower the coffin to the bottom of the hole. The boards were removed. As the coffin sank out of sight the preacher intoned: "Lord, we commit the mortal remains of our brother into the earth; and his soul in thy keeping."

Doc stooped and picked up a handful of loose earth and dropped it on top of the coffin. Opie followed. One by one, the rest of the funeral party did likewise.

Which one did so with fingers washed in Jim's blood? Which one?

Opie and Doc linked arms and began the long, slow walk back from the cemetery.

Finally Opie said: "You spoke a nice piece, Dr. Killian."

"I tried." Doc was gruff, raw from the loss of his friend. If he hadn't gotten Jim mixed up in the hunt, this funeral wouldn't have been held. In a way Doc felt like a killer, but he knew Jim wouldn't have wanted that.

"I think Jim would have liked what you said," Opie said slowly. Her hand was warm, comforting. "He never was much on pious words or formal phrases. He was just a common man who did what he could in an uncommon way. We'll all miss him." She looked up into Doc's face. "We need someone to replace him, be a friend to man as the phrase goes. How about you?"

Doc halted. At the moment he certainly didn't feel friendly to a whole lot of folks. "What do you mean, Opie?"

"We need a resident philosopher. A person we can all tell our troubles to in our hour of need."

Doc gripped Opie by the shoulders. "I'll tell you one thing I'm going to do."

"What's that?"

"I'm going to find out who killed Jim."

Opie looked scared, but she nodded. "I guess you have to," she said softly. "Be careful, Doc."

Chapter 15

Doc went back to the blacksmith shop. The front doors were still locked as Amos had left them the day before. Doc went around to the back door. Locked. It didn't matter. What he'd come to see were the tracks that led from the forge to the funeral parlor. He knelt down to peer at them. They were still fresh enough to be seen as hardly anyone had walked in the back alley way.

Actually there were four sets. He and Amos had made two sets when they were following the trail from where they found Jim's body back to the shop. The other tracks were made by Jim's dragging heels and the killer, who had walked backwards while dragging Jim's body. Evidently he'd grasped Jim's body under the armpits, lifted most of the weight, but let the heels drag. The killer's prints had the same "run down at the heel" marks Doc had seen twice before.

One thing still puzzled Doc. How had Jim had time to write his message? As Amos had speculated, the killer must not have moved Jim's body immediately after striking him down, must have been distracted and left long enough for Jim to crawl around the anvil and write his message. Where had the murderer gone while Jim was doing that?

Doc went back around to the front doors of the forge. Sure enough, a few of the killer's bootprints led out into the street before they were lost in the multitude of other tracks that covered the dusty surface. There were also a few prints that showed where two sets of the killer's tracks led into the blacksmith shop. They were indistinct, but Doc puzzled them out.

The murderer must have knifed Jim, left him for a bit, went

out the front doors, came back, dragged Jim out the back door and stuck him in the coffin at the undertaking parlor. The other set of tracks leading into the forge must have been made when the murderer followed Jim inside.

Doc had hit another dead end. It was impossible to follow the killer's trail in the much-used surface of the main street. For whatever reason, the man had gone into the street and returned the same way. This could only mean that the killer was well known in town, felt safe in walking around in plain sight, even when he had a corpse waiting for him in the smithy.

A cool bastard. Cold-blooded. Doc's scalp prickled, but the fear twisting his guts was overcome by bitter anger. Whoever the killer was, Doc meant to find him.

Backtracking, Doc went behind the undertaking parlor and considered the trail. The killer's tracks went backwards into the parlor and didn't come out again. This had to mean the killer put Jim's body on display and calmly left by the front door. Only a man of iron nerve would play such a game, someone commonly seen along the main street.

Who? Bob Noel? Big Bill?

"I hope you're having better luck with your tracking than I did."

Doc whirled at the voice and reached for his gun. Deputy Sid Harris thrust his arms out before him.

"Hold on there, Doc! It's only me."

Only then did Doc realize his pocket was empty. Amos still had his derringer. He'd have to remember to get that back. "You got to be careful coming up behind a man like that, Sid. Way things are around here I'm liable to shoot first and ask questions later. That is, if Amos ever gives me my gun back," he concluded ruefully.

Sid whistled in relief at Doc's empty hand. "I lucked out that time. Next time I'll whistle when I'm within a hundred feet of you."

"What about your tracking?" Doc demanded. "In all the excitement I forgot to ask you what you found out when you went off after Bill's bushwhacker."

Sid shuffled his feet. He seemed embarrassed. "I didn't find out nothing."

"Where'd the tracks go, Sid?"

The deputy stooped down and drew a rough map in the dust with his finger. "Here's the river. Tracks run back into the brush for a ways, then double along the river to the crossing. I picked them up the other side of the river and they just came back to town." Sid stood up. "Well, not the man tracks. I found where he got on his horse back in the brush. It was the horse tracks I followed back to town."

"Where did you track the horse to?"

Sid pointed through the gap between the buildings. "Main Street. They got mixed up with all the other tracks. Whoever shot Bill rode right into town as big as you please."

The bushwhacker was a mighty cool character. Was he Jim's killer, too? If so, that cleared Bill. Evidently, like the killer, the bushwhacker was so well known around town that he could do almost anything and remain undetected. It was going to be rough to isolate him from his background. Somehow, Doc had to make this man visible. Sid suddenly remembered his errand.

"Say, the reason I came looking for you is that Bill's regained consciousness. Amos sent me for you."

"Bill said anything yet?" Doc asked eagerly.

"No. He'd just come to when I left." Sid grinned. "He and his wife were kind of having a reunion. Let's get back there! I'm sure hankering to hear what Bill was doing when he got shot."

"You and me both," said Doc.

They hurried down the main street to Doc's home office. Amos was waiting out front for them.

"Why ain't you inside questioning Bill?" Doc wanted to know.

Amos pointed a thumb towards the office. "I wanted Bill and Heather to have a minute to themselves when he came awake. Besides, I figured you would want to be there when he started talking."

As the three men came through the office door, they could hear Big Bill talking and Heather crying.

"Come on, Heather," Bill's words were low and soft, "tell me what you're crying about."

Heather sniffed. "Because I'm so happy, you big hunk of cheese. What do you mean by riding out of town and getting yourself shot? I thought I might have to go back to working for a living for myself."

"Aw, now Heather." Bill's voice broke. He cleared his throat and gasped out his teasing. "You know I wouldn't die on you just because I stopped a little ol' bitty piece of lead."

Amos, Doc, and Sid came into the room. "Hello, boys," Bill said weakly, raising his eyebrows. "What are you doing here? Holding a wake or a celebration? Seems like the least you could do is supply some whiskey and some music."

"You got any whiskey?" Amos asked Doc. Doc went to a cupboard to find a bottle. "You got to supply the music," Amos continued. "For starters why don't you compose a ballad about where you were headed when you got shot."

Doc came back with the bottle. He handed it to Bill. The blacksmith pulled the cork with his teeth and spat it out on the floor, shakily tilted up the half-filled bottle and took a long gulp. "Much obliged, Doc. That little whistle wetter will have to do until I can get a real drink. But I'm obliged for the sample."

"Cut out the comedy, Bill," said Amos. "You're under suspicion of having killed Jim Balinte. Did you?"

Bill's eyes widened. He stifled a cry, then looked long and hard at the sheriff. "Up to this minute I didn't know Jim was dead," he said slowly, moving his head as though dazed. "Why, he was in my shop not long before I went on that wild-goose chase. He came in, looked around, acted like he was reading sign on my floor. I asked him what he was doing, but he said it was private. Pretty soon he went over to the livery stable. I didn't kill him. You know better than that, Amos. He was my friend." Bill's voice rose from the low monotone in which he

had been speaking. "Why would anyone, let alone me, want to kill Jim?"

"I wish I knew," Amos replied harshly. "Somebody stuck a knife in him, at your forge, put his body on display in the funeral parlor window. Sid saw you hightailing it out of town about the time all this happened. If you didn't do it, where were you going when that bullet knocked you out of the saddle?"

"I was going to repair a wagon."

There was a moment of unbelieving silence in the room.

"In the middle of the night?" Amos asked incredulously.

Bill sucked saliva to wet his dry throat. "Why, hell, Amos. I left before dark. It was a rush job. Word came in that some folks had busted their wagon crossing the river. The woman was close to having a baby. They said for me to hurry so they could get her in here to Doc."

Amos demanded sharply, "Who sent for you?"

"I don't know."

The sheriff stared at Bill skeptically. "You mean to tell me you rushed out of town in the late evening and didn't even know who sent for you?"

"That's right, Sheriff. Happens all the time." Bill paused to gather his strength. "Word gets passed that somebody's in trouble and I go rescue them. I'm sometimes called the local St. Bernard dog. Only this trip, instead of getting paid in whiskey, I got paid off in lead."

"Who brought the word to you?"

"Frank Kimbrough. Bryce's night man. He told me there was a broken wagon at the crossing. I don't know where he heard it." Bill closed his eyes. He still looked weak and pale. "Like I told you, it happens all the time. I go do what I can."

"What happened after you reached the crossing?" Doc asked.

Bill tried to sit up. Pain convulsed his face. Heather quietly pushed him back. "There wasn't nobody there," he said. "I thought maybe I'd got mixed up and didn't understand where the wagon would be. I headed upstream a ways to see if I could

find it." His eyes turned to Doc. "How long have I been out?"

"About twenty-four hours." Doc wanted to believe the good-natured giant. He almost did. Almost. "We buried Jim this afternoon. Did you know he got killed in your shop?"

"That's what Amos just said. I didn't know anything about it." Bill was silent for a moment, eyes glittering as if in grief for his friend. "All I know is I didn't kill him and he wasn't in my forge when I left. You can ask Frank about that."

Amos turned to Sid. "Bring Frank over here."

Sid left and Amos turned back to Bill. "Did you notice anything just before you got shot? See anybody? Hear any noise?"

"Nope. Just me and clear blue sky and the river." Bill grinned weakly. "I was riding along, minding my own business, when wham! Felt like somebody had smacked me in the back with a twenty-pound sledge. Funny thing. It hurt like hell when the bullet first hit and then I just sort of floated for a while."

The giant's eyes got a faraway look in them. "Did you ever dream where you were running through the fields on a windy fall day? You know, the kind of a dream where you float along real slow like? No matter how hard you run, you just go slow and easy, take giant steps and it seems like you could fly if you just flapped your arms hard enough. It was like that for a little while. Then I blacked out." He rested a moment, swallowed, and went on. "Don't remember another thing until I woke up and found ol' crybaby slobbering over me." He encircled Heather's waist with one great arm. She moved over close to him.

At that moment Sid came back with Frank. The sheriff gave the man a hard look. "Frank, Bill says you told him there was a broken wagon at the crossing yesterday evening."

"That's right," Frank gulped. "I told him about the wagon."

The sheriff moved closer to Frank. A note of menace crept into his voice. "How did you know about the wagon in the first place?"

Frank backed away. "A kid came into the livery stable and

told me," he faltered. "Not a little boy, but a young punk waddie."

"Know who he was?" Amos' tone of voice implied that Frank was lying.

"Never saw him before in my life, Sheriff." The livery man was sweating now. "He was a young cowpoke. Had the look of a drifter. I guess he'd just come into town to get drunk and passed the broken-down wagon on the way. I haven't seen him around since."

"Did you see Jim Balinte around the forge before Bill left?" Amos snapped.

Frank pulled a bandana out and mopped his brow. "No, I didn't. Bill lit right out when I told him about the wagon, and how the lady was about to have a baby. Jim wasn't around then. It wasn't until I got back to the livery stable that I saw him again."

"Whaaat?" gasped Amos and Doc in unison.

They both advanced on Frank.

Frank took a short step backwards and held up his hands as though to ward off a blow. "I said Jim was at the livery stable when I got back. He was in the front office talking to Mr. Collins. It was almost time for Mr. Collins to go home for the day." Frank's words came out in a nervous rush.

"They talked for a little while and then Jim went out and headed down the street towards the jail. Mr. Collins got on his horse and rode out the other way. I went back and started mucking out the stalls. That's all I know!" Frank ran out of words and breath at the same instant, gazed at them imploringly.

The sheriff and Doc exchanged glances. "Then it looks like Bryce was the last man to see Jim alive," said Amos. "Get on back to the stable, Frank. Thanks for talking to us."

"Glad to oblige, Sheriff." Frank was greatly relieved to be dismissed. He started backing out of the office. "Wish I could tell you more. But that's all I know." He fled.

Amos looked at Big Bill and Heather. The blacksmith lay on the bed with his arm about his wife. Amos cleared his throat.

"Guess that clears you, Bill. You just take it easy here." He motioned for Doc and Sid to follow and started into Doc's kitchen.

"One thing, Amos," Bill called after them, "when you boys track down that bushwhacker, I want a word or two with him. In private. Out back of my shop. I've got something to give him." Bill slowly held up his fists.

As soon as the men got into Doc's kitchen, Amos said: "Sid, I hate to keep sending you out to fetch people, but I sure would like to talk to Bryce tonight. Would you mind trying to find him?"

"No problem, Amos. He's probably at the saloon having his evening drink." The deputy disappeared.

Amos and Doc sat down at the kitchen table. Amos had grown haggard the past few days. Probably hadn't been sleeping too well. There were circles under his eyes and his face had a strained look.

Well, for that matter, Doc probably looked pretty much the same way himself. Jim's death, Big Bill getting bushwhacked, the killer still free. Plenty for them both to worry about. Funny how you never really looked at your friends. You saw them everyday and didn't notice they were getting older. They just seemed to stay the same until one day you got to looking at yourself in the mirror and realized there were lines in your face and your hair had turned gray. Then you looked at your friends again. Sure enough, they'd aged right along with you.

It was always a shock for Doc to see his face in the shaving mirror in the morning. He never thought of himself as being fifty years old. Inside he still looked at the world through sixteen-year-old eyes. His thoughts were much the same. He still had a lively interest in the world. But when he saw his mirrored image, he realized time was creeping up on him. Just as it was on Amos.

The two men sat in silence while the moments passed. Doc had a pendulum clock on his kitchen wall that ticked off the seconds with its rhythmic swing. "Tic-tock, tic-tock." Each arc of the pendulum sent a small shock of sound surging through the clock case, down the board wall, across the floorboards, up the wooden chair legs, and into the consciousness of the men. With each tick of the clock, with each beat of their hearts, the rhythm repeated. "Time-goes. Time-goes. Time-goes." And so it did. Time went on until Sid came back with Bryce.

"Come in, Bryce," said the sheriff. "Sid, you better go out and make the night rounds." Bryce came into the kitchen. Sid left for his duties.

Amos motioned Bryce to a chair. "Frank tells me you and Jim were talking in your office shortly before he was killed."

"That's right." Bryce's clear gray-green eyes moved from Amos to Doc.

"Would you mind telling us what you were talking about?"

"Nothing in particular. Everything in general." Bryce was nonchalant. "He just dropped by to pass the time of day. We talked about the weather. How hot it was. He mentioned business had been slow at his place. I told him it was slow with me too. That's how we talked. Just conversation."

"Where did Jim go when he left your place?"

"He started down the street towards the jail."

"And where did you go?" the quiet, relentless voice pursued.

"I rode out to the edge of town to see a friend." Bryce's neck colored. "You may as well know. It was a lady friend. I'd rather not say who."

Softly, ever so softly, the sheriff asked his most important question. "Then Jim was alive the last time you saw him?"

"He sure was, Amos!" Bryce leaned forward in his chair. "From the direction he was heading I thought he might be going to see you. I didn't pay much attention. Had other things on my mind and I was late."

"Do you have any idea who killed Jim?"

"No."

The sheriff's voice became louder. "Or who bushwhacked Bill?"

"No." Bryce's spine stiffened and his tone was clipped. "I just know it wasn't me. Either case."

"You're not much help, Bryce," grunted Amos. "But thanks anyway."

"Guess I better get back to my drinking." Bryce rose, hesitated. "I can tell you the name of the woman I was with, in confidence, if you have to check my story."

"No," said the sheriff. "Reckon that's not necessary."

"Glad to hear that. 'Night gentlemen." Bryce moved gracefully out of the house.

"There's something a little too smooth about Bryce's story," Doc grumbled. "I got a feeling he didn't tell the truth about his conversation with Jim."

"May be." Amos lifted thin eyebrows. "But why lie about that? It'd be easy enough to find out who the woman was that he claimed to be with when Jim got killed. I think he was probably talking straight."

Amos paused and doggedly let Doc have it. "I do think your nerves are getting on edge. You're starting to doubt everything again. Why don't you try and get some rest?"

Doc smiled ruefully. "I was thinking the same about you, Amos. You're probably right. I seem to be worn down to where I'm suspicious of everyone. All right. I'm going to go to bed."

Amos got up and left. Doc went with him to the front door and locked it. He flinched as he passed his front window. Hell of a note to fear getting shot at in your own house.

But that's the way things were.

Chapter 16

Doc woke up once in the early morning hours, looked at his watch, rolled over, and went back to sleep. When he finally got out of bed at noon he felt better. His body at least was refreshed from the long sleep, though his mind was still in turmoil.

Nothing had been solved. None of his five prime suspects seemed to be the man he sought, though he still wondered about Bob Noel.

Now Jim had been killed. As he sat nursing his coffee, Doc was overtaken with listlessness. He didn't feel like doing anything. His will for action was paralysed. Cup after cup of coffee went down his throat as he sat and tried to dredge up some clue, some hint of the killer's identity. If he'd been a drinking man, he'd have gotten drunk.

As it was, he moodily wasted away the whole afternoon and drank a pot of coffee by himself. His brain seemed numbed and his thoughts chased each other in vain circles. He finally became aware that someone was shaking him, and he came out of his reverie with a start. Opie was standing in front of him.

"You all right?" Opie demanded, blue eyes concerned.

"Yeh. I'm fine."

"For a minute or two there I thought you was dead." Opie took hold of his hand. "C'mon. Get up. Ain't you ready yet?"

"Uh—ready for what?" Doc blinked.

Opie dropped his hand and observed him with mock despair. "Heavens to Betsey! Do you mean to sit there and say I plumb forgot to tell you about the play party? Must have slipped my mind. Tonight's the play party at the school."

"What's a play party?" mumbled Doc.

Opie regarded him with amusement. "Don't you know nothin'? That's a party where folks play games, and dance, and have a good time, and do other things. I thought about putting it off on account of Jim, but he'd want us to have something to cheer people up. You're elected to be my escort. C'mon, wrangler. Let's move it out."

"Opie, I don't feel like going to no play party. Go along without me. I'm not cleaned up or dressed proper."

"Won't take you but a minute. Where do you keep your spare pants?" Opie started up the stairs to his bedroom.

"Hold on there!" Doc jumped from his chair. "I can find my own pants. Wait here and I'll get dressed."

Opie came back down the stairs and sat demurely on the settee.

Doc freshened up and changed his clothes, pulled on a hand-tooled pair of light-weight boots. Doc had big feet. He couldn't wear standard-sized shoes. All his footwear was custom-made. Sometimes he took a lot of kidding about his feet. His friends were always saying he'd be a good-sized man if there wasn't so much of him turned under.

"Man alive." Opie gave a short whistle. "Look at the dude, will ya? I'm gonna have a lot of the girls mad at me tonight. Just wait 'til they see me coming in on the arm of that good-looking clothes horse. I'll have to scratch eyes and pull hair the rest of the night just to keep them hussies off you."

Doc chuckled. "Quit that, Opie. You make me feel like a fool."

"We don't want nobody thinking that. Do we feller? Not just from looking at you, anyhow."

They left the house and started towards the schoolhouse. As usual, Opie took Doc's arm. It seemed natural. They fitted together real good.

"If it's not too much to ask," Doc asked, "just what particular kind of a play party is this going to be?"

Opie's laugh reminded Doc of rippling water. "We need to raise money for school furnishings and supplies. We could have just gone around for cash donations but we haven't had a party in a long time. The women of Gila Crossing need to get into some fancy duds and play glamorous."

Opie let go of Doc's arm and waltzed a few steps by herself, turning graceful circles to imaginary music. Doc smiled. It was good to see her enjoying herself.

"You got no idea, Doc, how deadly dull it is being a house-wife and mother. Play parties keep about half the women in town from going stark raving mad. Most of them stay right on the verge. Yep. In a real live town like Gila Crossing the best thing they ever invented was the play party."

The schoolhouse sat on the edge of town, the site deliber-ately chosen so the children had plenty of space to run and play and holler. That last reason was probably the most impor-tant. The schoolhouse and play yard were located several good hollers away from the nearest residence.

Like most schoolhouses of its day and place, this one was a large, one-room building of adobe. It had a wood-shingled gable roof, large windows along the side walls, a double front door and a flag pole in the front yard. Two small privies were out back, and next to the school was a decrepit bell tower.

Some forgotten schoolmaster, perhaps thinking of a previous life on the Atlantic sea coast, had built the tower like a light-house. Its rickety frame had been boarded in with clapboard siding. A makeshift staircase wound up the inside of the tower to end in a platform at the top.

Up in the belfry, instead of a warning beacon, hung a mas-sive bell. This bell had come from an abandoned church and must have weighed a ton.

The rope that rang the bell descended through a hole in the belfry platform and extended to ground level. Opie was the only one who pulled the rope, keeping a wary eye out for fear that she might cause the whole tower to collapse.

Unbeknownst to the adults of the community, the tower had become a forbidden place of awe to the children. Many a boy had been prodded into proving his incipient manhood by climbing the tower. Amidst the jeers of his peers, at least once at the beginning of each school year, some trembling hero climbed to the bell platform. It was an experience seldom repeated by even the most valiant.

By the time Doc and Opie reached the schoolhouse, the party had already started. Most townspeople had walked to the party. There was a light sprinkling of horses and wagons tethered along the schoolyard fence. Inside there was light, laughter, and the sound of many voices.

Desks were arranged along the sides of the room leaving a bare space in the center.

Up front on the teacher's desk and some other tables were rows of pies and cakes to be auctioned off for the fund raising. There were also pots of coffee, sandwiches, potato salad, pickles, and cans of milk for those who didn't drink coffee.

The only surprising thing about the appearance of the schoolhouse was the lack of children. The little ones had been left at home with older sisters and brothers so that mothers and fathers could have a night off and enjoy their play party unencumbered by the usual duties of parenthood.

There was a festive mood to the gathering in spite of Jim's death. They had buried him and would mourn him a long time in their hearts, but death was common on the frontier and you took fun when you found it. Much gossip was being traded by the women. The men were busy lying to one another and occasionally slipping off in small groups to go outside and rummage in the wagons where some of the more provident of their numbers had been foresighted enough to provide remedy in case of snakebite.

Doc and Opie slowly worked their way through the crowd, greeting friends and acquaintances along the way. "Hey, Opie," called Bryce from a group of women. "Who's the big dude you got with you?"

"Some drummer that came in on the evening stage," said Opie. "He wanted to know where all the wild night life was so I naturally brought him along."

"Hope he's no boot salesman." Bryce gave his companions a sly wink. "It'd take two men and a boy to wear that pair he's got on." Doc's laugh boomed out with the rest.

"Don't know how you guessed my business," he said. "These aren't my stock-in-trade I'm wearing. I threw the boots away. These are the packing cases I've got on." He and Opie moved on to where Amos Dalton was deep in conversation. "Howdy, Sheriff," said Doc.

"Hello, Doc. Hello, Opie." Amos greeted them. "Nice night for a party."

"Sure is," Doc nodded. "Only thing is, seems to be a loud-mouthed pickpocket standing over there with that group of women." He pointed over to Bryce. "Wish you'd keep an eye on him before he steals something valuable."

"Don't think he can get away with anything they don't want him to have," chuckled Amos. He turned back to his friends.

Doc and Opie finally got to the front of the room where the food was laid out under the vigilant eyes of Bob Noel and his wife Ruth.

Ruth asked Opie: "Didn't you bring anything for the auction?"

"I sent a pecan pie over earlier. I didn't want to have to carry it while walking with this impetuous fool." Opie made a face at Doc. "A girl don't never know when she's gonna need both hands to defend herself when she's out with a guy like him."

"Why Doctor," smiled Ruth, "I didn't know you were that kind of a man."

"Ordinarily I'm not," protested Doc, "but when you're out with Opie, anything can, and most often does, happen."

"Isn't that nice?" Ruth laughed musically. "I can remember when I used to need both hands to fend off Robert. Not lately though. He's become quite reserved in recent years. Ah, but the old days. Things were different then." She gazed at her husband with affection.

Could this man possibly be a killer? Doc looked closely at Noel.

"Just because there's snow on the roof doesn't mean there still isn't a fire in the furnace," said Noel patting his gray hair. He gave his wife a hug.

"Now Robert," Ruth colored, though she was pleased by the

attention. "You stop that! Isn't it time for you to start seeing about the auction?"

"You the auctioneer tonight?" asked Doc.

"Yup," said Noel. He smiled at Opie. "How's Doc going to know which pie to buy?"

"I'll give him a good nudge."

"Guess I better start then." Noel hopped up on a chair and clapped his hands. "All right, folks. Step right up here to the front. The auction is about to begin."

People stopped their talking and crowded around the front of the room. Bob picked up a pie and began his chant. "Here's a good-smelling apple pie. What am I offered? I've got two bits. Who'll make it thirty cents? Thirty, thirty—and thirty-five! Thank you. I've got thirty-five and asking forty. Forty? Forty going once, going twice—and sold to that lucky man for forty cents. Now here is a lovely cake. Who'll go forty cents on this delectable concoction of the baker's art?"

The auction proceeded smoothly as reluctant husbands, at wifely urgings, bid the pastry up as high as their wallets could stand. When Opie's pecan pie came on the auction block, Bryce bid against Doc. Between the two of them the pie was finally knocked down at the unheard of bid of one dollar. Doc's was the winning bid. He took quite a bit of joshing from the crowd about paying such a preposterous price.

"Doc must think he's gonna get his money's worth out of that pie," yelled one voice.

"He will with Opie thrown in for boot," said another.

Through all the good-natured ribbing Doc and Opie just laughed at one another and their friends. As the auctioning resumed, Doc said to Opie: "Let's go outside for a breath of fresh air. It's getting a mite warm in here for me."

"Anything you say," rejoined Opie with a twinkle in her eye. "Them boys is gonna keep on kidding you like that until you make an honest woman of me."

Doc and Opie walked away from the lights of the schoolhouse windows and stood in the shadow of the bell tower. Before them spread the vastness of the open desert. No moon was out. Only the dim starlight enabled them to see one another. The wind was blowing in short, hard gusts.

It was much cooler than inside the crowded schoolhouse.

"See anything you like?" Opie asked Doc.

"What?" Doc's attention came back from wherever it had wandered. "Oh, sorry, Opie. I must have been thinking about something else."

"Seems to me like you've been in a trance all day. A penny for your thoughts."

Doc grinned wryly. "I was just wondering how it is that a woman of your education and occupation manages to talk so common."

"My good Dr. Killian. Does it incommode your intellectual processes when you note that a paragon of virtue and model of decorum such as I should revert to the common vernacular in mundane conversation with mere mortals?"

"Huh?" said Doc. "Yeh. I guess that's what I mean, all right. Only I don't think I'd ever put it quite in that particular manner."

"Just goes to show, my friend, that you can take the girl out of the country, but you can't take the country out of the girl. I come from common stock. My folks were good, down-to-earth, common people. My earliest speech patterns were those of country talk. I was the first of my family to ever graduate from high school."

Opie leaned against the tower. "When I left the farm and went off to college my father had to sell ten head of cattle to give me enough money to matriculate. Cattle he really couldn't afford to sell. I worked my way through college as a waitress in a boardinghouse. I fit in well as a waitress. I spoke the language of the other boarders. We understood each other."

Opie smiled briefly at the memory. Then her face hardened. "But when I attended classes at the school I learned I was the country bumpkin come to town. The first time I ever stood up to recite in class I had the other students rolling in the aisles. And I hadn't even said anything funny!"

Opie crossed her arms over her breast. She spoke in grim earnest. "It was a great lesson. I kept my mouth shut until I'd learned to talk like the rest of the educated snobs in my classes. And all the time I hated them! Hated them because they'd laughed at a poor dumb country girl who'd never had their chances. I signed up for all the elocution courses the college offered, stayed awake nights studying grammar books. I spent hours standing in front of a mirror mouthing the speech patterns of educated talk. It got so bad that the other boarders quit talking to me because they couldn't understand what I was saying."

Doc started to say something, but she cut him off. "I kept right at it. I was going to show those college snots a thing or two. In four years time I could talk like an educated young lady to the manor born. I was class valedictorian. Gave a commencement address so full of multisyllable words and high-flung phrases that three fourths of the graduating seniors didn't know what I was talking about. I even had some of the faculty members scratching their heads."

Opie's voice quivered with bitter amusement. "And it was like ashes in my mouth. It wasn't me after all. It was a role I was taking, an act of snobbism to outsnob the snobs."

Doc nodded understandingly. "What happened after you finished college?"

"After graduation I came back home. I married a common man and started teaching common children in a common school. When I tried out some of my highfalutin language on the school kids they didn't laugh at me. No. They were dumbfounded. They couldn't understand what I was saying."

Opie unfolded her arms and took a step away from the tower. "So I've gone back to teaching in the vernacular. I talk to my pupils so they can understand me. I also do my best to upgrade their speech patterns. By the time they leave my school they can hold their own in the outside world." Opie laughed teasingly. "I don't talk quite as countrified at school as I do with you."

Doc was contrite. "Forgive me, Opie. I didn't mean to belittle you."

"I know you didn't." She patted his cheek. "It's just that when I'm with you I forget all my book learning and revert to plain old common me." She was joking, of course, but joking nice.

Suddenly, with an ominous crackle, the bell tower started to fall.

Doc looked up, saw the structure beginning to sway. For a moment time and motion seemed suspended. Slowly, ever so slowly, the belfry pushed past the point of equilibrium and started an arc of rapidly accelerating descent that would eventually crush them. Doc grabbed Opie and tried to jerk her to safety. He almost succeeded. As the tower crashed to the ground, he rolled free, but Opie's legs were pinned beneath the fallen mass of lumber and metal. Doc scrambled to his feet as people came pouring out of the schoolhouse. Opie was unconscious.

"Give me a hand!" yelled Doc. Hands and arms and backs and legs bent to the task of hoisting the twisted wreckage off Opie's legs. Men grunted, strained and lifted, until they moved the weight of the timbers enough for Doc to pull Opie out. He held her in his trembling arms, her head cradled against his pounding heart.

Opie's eyes fluttered and then opened. She looked up at Doc and said: "Looks like that last speech brought down the house."

Then she passed out again.

Chapter 17

Swiftly, Doc laid Opie down. Someone brought a lamp from the schoolhouse. Doc examined her legs, handling them as gently as he could.

One of them was broken. He called for splints and bandages as he removed Opie's shoes and stockings. Doc carefully set the broken bone, applied splints with the help of other people.

Mercifully, Opie didn't regain consciousness during the ordeal. Doc picked her up and carried Opie back to her house where neighbor women undressed her and put her to bed. Then Doc ordered everyone out of the house.

He placed a chair by Opie's bedside and spent the rest of the night dozing and waking by her side. She slept until the sun was high in the sky. When she woke and tried to move, a groan escaped her lips. Doc, who had drowsed off with the morning, woke up.

Opie gave Doc a weak grin. "Seems like every time I have a date with you something happens. What happened to my leg?"

"Your leg's broken. Don't try to move. Here, drink this."

Doc gave her a drink of water laced with a few drops of laudanum. There was no cure for her condition except rest. Fortunately the skin on her legs had not been broken. Aside from massive bruising and the broken bone she was all right. But, she might run a high fever. An elevated temperature usually came in cases like this, but Doc had a few medicines in his kit that could break a fever.

Soon the narcotic took effect and Opie drifted off to sleep. Just before she closed her eyes again she whispered something. Doc bent over her.

"What did you say?" he asked.

She smiled. Without opening her eyes she repeated: "I love you."

She looked like a young girl. Doc gently pulled the cover over her and sat for a moment listening to her even breathing. He was sorry she was hurt, but it made him feel good to take care of her.

Amos Dalton and a neighbor lady named Mrs. Mognette came into the sickroom. They tiptoed up to the sick bed. "How is she?" asked Amos.

"I just gave her something to make her sleep. She's strong and healthy. She'll come out of it all right."

"Mrs. Mognette will watch over Opie for a spell." Amos motioned for Doc to get up. "Come with me. I've got something to show you."

Doc told Mrs. Mognette what to do when Opie woke up and left a bottle of medicine. Mrs. Mognette promised to send for him as soon as Opie roused.

"What do you want to show me?" Doc asked Amos wearily as they stepped outside. He was bone tired.

"You'll see," said Amos. "That bell tower didn't fall of its own accord. Somebody deliberately pushed it over. You're lucky to be alive this morning."

Doc felt the skin on the back of his neck tighten up. Rage swept over him. First Jim! Now another try at him that could have killed Opie!

"Any sign of who did the pushing?" he rasped.

"Your old friend. The guy with the run-down heel."

When they reached the fallen tower, Amos pointed out the deep tracks made by Doc's enemy. It was plain to see where the man had braced his back against the tower and pushed hard enough to topple it over. The telltale worn-down right heel mark was deeply embedded in the soft dirt. Doc's blood raced. He forgot his fatigue. "Amos, let's track this man down right now! I'm sick and tired of him running around loose."

"Easier said than done," Amos scowled. "As usual, the trail's stomped out by all the other footprints of people who were here last night."

"Amos, we know that whoever made these boot marks killed Jim. He also bushwhacked Bill. He took a shot at me through the front window one night. The owner of these tracks listened in on a conversation I had with Opie. The owner of this track is probably the man who killed Jeanne. He lives here. His coming and going is so common that nobody notices him. I propose to walk every inch of this town and keep looking until I find some fresh tracks made by this worn-down boot heel."

Amos seemed to withdraw into himself at Doc's barrage.

"All right," he said tiredly. "Let's head back for the center of town."

The men started along the schoolhouse street, scanning the dust of the road. They passed Opie's house, Bob Noel's house, and the courthouse. As they came near the end of the street a man turned the corner and came towards them.

"Here comes Bryce," said Amos.

Doc looked up. "No. That's Frank Kimbrough."

They met in the middle of the dusty road.

"Good morning, Sheriff. Good morning, Dr. Killian." Frank's squeaky young voice was respectful.

The older men just stared at the young man. His tracks were plain to see in the dew-dampened morning dust. Frank Kimbrough's right-hand boot heel was making the track they sought. Suddenly Doc knew the meaning of Jim's last message.

"You're under arrest," said Amos reaching for his gun.

Frank looked behind him to see who the sheriff was talking to. There was no one there. Puzzled, he turned to face the two older men. "Were you talking to me, Sheriff?"

Amos' gun cleared leather. "Nobody else. Let's get over to the jail."

"But, Sheriff," stammered Frank, "what are you arresting me for?"

"For the murder of Jim Balinte and trying to kill Doc and Opie last night. Are you coming peaceably?"

"I never did nothing! You must be kidding!" Frank's voice rose. "Tell me you're joshing!"

"You're wasting my time." Amos took Frank by the arm, roughly turned him around and marched him to the jail. Doc followed. When they got into the office, Amos spun the young man into a chair.

"Pull off your boots," the sheriff ordered.

"Do what?" Frank quavered.

Amos grabbed his right leg and pulled off the boot. There was the rounded heel that had been making the tracks Doc had seen too many times.

"I never figured you for a low-down coyote that would kill Jim Balinte," said Amos. "Just goes to show it's about time for me to hang up my gun. Here you been working right next door to my office all this time and I never even suspected you."

"I tell you, I didn't do it!" yelled Frank.

"Then how come your boot tracks were along the trail where Jim's body was dragged from the blacksmith shop to the funeral parlor?" demanded Amos.

"And it was your tracks I found across the street from the house the morning after someone took a shot at me," hammered Doc.

"Last night," Frank whimpered protestively, but Amos went on, tight lipped, "When you tipped over the bell tower and almost killed Doc and Opie, you left another good set of tracks. You might as well admit it, Frank. Save us all a lot of trouble."

"I didn't do none of those things, Sheriff," moaned Frank. His eyes flitted helplessly back and forth. He gulped for air and his face was ashen. "It wasn't me. It must have been somebody else."

The lawman's jaw muscles tightened. He backhanded Frank across the mouth. "Now. I'm going to ask you one more time. Did you kill Jim?"

"No!"

Amos drew back his arm to hit him with his doubled fist.

Doc reached over and grabbed the sheriff's arm. "It won't do any good to beat him to death." Amos dropped his arm.

"Did you kill my wife?" Doc asked Frank.

The young man trembled. "For the love of God, don't even say that! No, no, no! I didn't kill Jim, or your wife—or anyone!"

Amos stared at the prisoner in disgust. "Frank, you're going to be charged with murder. The penalty in this territory is to be hung by the neck until you slowly strangle to death. It's not a pleasant way to die. If you tell us what really happened when you killed Jim then I'll try to make a deal for you and get you off with a life sentence. If you keep on telling us this cock-and-bull story about being innocent, I'll help put the rope around your neck myself. What's it going to be?"

"I—I didn't do it, Sheriff." Frank was close to tears.

"All right. What you need is time locked up in a cell by yourself. When you've had time to think it over, you'll change your story."

"How am I going to change my story when I didn't do it?"

Amos jerked Frank out of his chair and marched him back to the cellblock, thrust him into the lockup, and slammed the door. "You won't be here long. As soon as the word gets out that you're the one who killed Jim some of the higher minded citizens of this town will probably find a rope of their own and save the government some money. I'm too old to face down a lynch mob. If I hear them coming, I just might make myself scarce around here." He locked the cell door.

Frank turned white and sat down heavily on the bunk bed. Amos came back out to the front office.

"Weren't you a little rough on him, Amos?" Doc asked.

"In this business you sometimes get better results if you throw the fear of God into these murdering punks. They all claim they're innocent. And if they keep on saying they are, long enough and loud enough, sometimes enough bleeding hearts on the jury get to feeling sorry for them and turn them loose." Amos strode rapidly up and down the office floor.

"The only real evidence we've got against Frank are his heel marks at the scene of the crime. It's purely circumstantial. If he gets real lucky, can find himself a slick lawyer and a weak-minded jury, we probably couldn't pin the rap on him. And he's one I'd like to see at the end of a rope."

"Don't try to beat a confession out of him, Amos."

"My God, Doc! You sound just like Jim used to talk. Are we talking about the same thing? I thought you wanted to find out who killed your wife and best friend."

"I do." Doc's voice was clear, calm, and deliberate. "But not by physically abusing a helpless man. If he's the one we're looking for, I'll gladly buy the rope to hang him. But we've got to be sure he is the right man. I know mistakes can happen. I've been in that same cell."

Amos flushed. He sat down in his chair and passed his hands over his face. Finally he looked at Doc. "Thanks for reminding me. In the heat of the moment I got kind of carried away."

Doc touched his friend's shoulder. "Let's leave the whole thing rest a while. I'm going to take a walk and do some thinking." Doc left the jail and stopped by Opie's house to see how she was getting along. She hadn't waked up. Mrs. Mognette assured Doc that another woman would relieve her in due time. There was nothing he could do there. Doc continued down the street. Soon he came to the schoolhouse.

No one was there. The twisted, broken wreckage lay where it had fallen. Frank's boot heel marks were still at the bottom of where the tower had stood. Doc looked again at the deep impressions. The right heel mark matched Frank's worn boot. There could be no mistake. Moving over a few feet Doc could see the spot where he had pulled Opie out from under the tower. His heart was heavy. It seemed as though he had brought nothing but trouble to other people.

First Jeanne, then Jim, now Opie. Moving blindly, not caring where his steps carried him, Doc came at last to the cemetery.

Doc hadn't been to the burying ground since Jim's funeral. He'd purposely avoided going there because Jeanne was also there, buried while Doc was locked up awaiting trial. No one had asked him if he wanted to go to her funeral, even told him about it until it was all over. He was still bitter about that. Since his return to Gila Crossing he hadn't been ready to accept the finality of her death by visiting her grave. Now he knew why he had wandered out to the cemetery.

At last he was ready.

Slowly, he walked through the cemetery. He didn't know where Jeanne was buried. No one had told him. Reading first one headstone, and then another, he worked his way up and down the rows until he found the spot.

It was a common-looking grave like all the others. A rounded mound of dirt. A gray stone marker. The headstone was one that Doc had ordered through Jim Balinte. He'd written the undertaker while locked up at the prison and sent money for the stone. At the top of the marker was a simple legend.

HERE LIES JEANNE KILLIAN
BELOVED WIFE OF V. E. KILLIAN
BORN 1839 – DIED 1876

Underneath the statistics was a short poem. It was one that Doc had written for Jeanne shortly before they were married.

Wide, wide are the meadows
Deep, deep are the skies.
But neither wide, nor deep shall keep
The light that lights your eyes;
From shining forth in splendored rays
From the depths, where love's light lies—
Wide, wide are the meadows
Deep, deep are the skies.

Doc sank to his knees and stared fixedly at the tombstone. Such futile words to try and convey the essence of Jeanne's life force. Mere words could never give an inkling as to the magnificent spirit of his wife. She was fairy princess and Earth Mother all wrapped up together in one free, limitless soul. Her zest for life shone like a beacon for all the lost souls of this world. She loved life and used it every day to bring joy into the hearts of others.

No one who knew her could doubt that life was worth living. Sadness couldn't last in her presence. Her compassion for people less fortunate than herself was boundless. No one ever approached her in need and went away empty-handed. Some sought material things, others things of the spirit. Jeanne gave to each according to their needs.

But most of all she was all things to him. She had been his helpmate. His Adam's rib, alter ego, conscience, guide. *My friend. My lover. My very dearest companion—my wife.*

What a small stone marked her last resting place. And yet it didn't matter. A stone the size of the pyramids wouldn't be big enough to record the truth of her existence. No stone at all would still not obscure the essence of her life.

This plot of ground would forever hold more than just Jeanne's remains. Here a part of his heart lay buried, never to be resurrected. That part of him that belonged to Jeanne had perished with her. No matter what course his life took from this moment on, he would never be completely whole though his mind and spirit could finally accept the fact of her death.

Doc remained kneeling by the grave for a long while. The sun beat down, the wind blew, clouds drifted across the sky. Small dust devils skipped about the cemetery like lost souls seeking an exit from purgatory. Nothing disturbed Doc's reverie. He neither saw nor felt his physical surroundings. It was as though he were a disembodied spirit drifting through the cosmos in search of a better world. And in a way, he was.

"Dr. Killian," a voice called.

Doc returned to the present. He looked about him with unseeing eyes for a moment before focusing on a small boy standing on the other side of the grave.

Large, deep-brown eyes framed by a halo of soft, wavy blond hair regarded him. "What are you doing?" asked the boy.

"Thinking," Doc said simply.

"How's come you're sitting on your knees?"

"I seem to think better in this position, Martin."

"Well, you're mamma's gonna be mad atcha for gettin' dirt all over your pantlegs."

Doc smiled at the child. Here was life and reality talking to him in the voice of a boy. Martin remembered his mission.

"Mamma says for you to come to Miss Opie's house right away."

Doc jumped to his feet. "Is Miss Opie awake?"

"Don't know," said the lad. "When Mamma says go, I git. You better come, too."

Doc followed the small messenger out of the graveyard. When they came to the gate, Doc turned back and softly said: "Good-bye, Jeanne."

Chapter 18

Doc and his guide soon arrived at Opie's house and went up to the sick room. "Hello, Opie," said Doc. He got no response. Mrs. Mognette took Martin and left the room. Doc pulled up a chair and sat beside the bed. He took Opie's hand and placed his fingers on her pulse. It was normal.

Still Opie said nothing. Doc relinquished the hand and replaced his pocket watch. The patient remained silent. Her eyes searched Doc's face. She seemed to be considering whether or not to speak before she turned her head away.

Doc reached out and touched her. "Are you in pain?"

"Some."

"Do you want me to give you something?"

"No."

"Look at me, Opie."

She did, rather defiantly.

"What's bothering you, Opie?" Doc asked in his best bedside manner.

"You."

"What do you mean?"

"Just that. You bother me."

Doc didn't know what to make of her. She might be suffering from shock, her mind might not be clear. Yet she seemed perfectly lucid. Life forces seemed to be normal. Her breathing was deep and regular. There was no sign of fever. Whatever pain she felt was at least bearable. She continued to look at him.

"I guess you're just going to have to tell me what troubles

you, Opie." Doc tried to give her a reassuring smile. "I'm a doctor, not a mind reader."

Opie started to speak, changed her mind, and turned away again.

This time Doc reached over with both hands, grasped her by the shoulders, and turned her to face him. "What do you think you're doing?"

"Minding my own business."

"Would you mind telling me what this is all about?"

"What for?" Opie replied. "You don't care about me. Why should I tell you anything?"

"Where did you get such an idea? Of course I care about you, Opie!"

"Enough to put your arms around me and welcome me back to life? Or am I just another patient to you?"

"I'm sorry, Opie. It didn't occur to me to do that. I—I've just come back from the cemetery."

Her face twisted. "Enjoy your visit?"

"Not especially. But it was something I had to do. This is the first time I've seen Jeanne's grave."

"Still there, is it?"

Opie's almost heartless comments were so out of keeping with her usual good nature that it seemed as if he were talking to a stranger. Whatever was eating Opie had deep roots. "You might as well spit it out and be done with it," he told her. "I don't understand what you're so upset about. But whatever it is, tell me so we'll both know."

"Upset? Who's upset?" Opie lashed back. "I always talk like this, or haven't you noticed?"

"You're not being very rational."

"What's there to be rational about? It's the irrational people who get what they want in this world."

Doc felt suddenly tired and old. "Opie—please."

"All right. I'll tell you what's on my mind. Is Jeanne still out there? Out at the cemetery?"

"Yes."

"Still dead?"

"Yes."

"Are you expecting any miracles? Think there's any chance she'll come back to life?"

"Of course she won't! Opie . . ."

"Then you admit she's dead and gone? Forever?"

"Yes."

"Then why don't you kiss me?"

"It—it just doesn't seem right to me yet."

"You can go straight to hell!" Opie looked at him levelly. "I don't want you hanging around me anymore. I've got other things to do with my life than waste it with a man who's still in love with a dream. And speaking of dreams; I had a dream. I dreamt that I told you I loved you."

"You didn't dream that. You told me."

"Then why aren't you laughing? Wasn't that funny?" Opie gave a short peal of laughter. "Just think. I dreamt I loved a man who loved a dream more than he loved life."

"You don't understand how it is, Opie," said Doc miserably.

"No. I guess I don't. I don't understand a man who prefers to live in the past. A man who doesn't believe life is for the living. I've told you before, Doc. I'll tell you again. You're not living!"

"Opie, please!" Doc reached out to touch her.

Her body stiffened. "Don't!" she muttered through clenched teeth. She turned to the wall.

Useless to try to talk with her in her present mood. He pushed back his chair and stood up. "I'll come back when you're feeling better."

There was no response from Opie. Her face remained turned to the wall. Cold, distant, aloof, she ignored him.

With a heavy heart Doc left the room. He told Mrs. Mognette to go back and stay with the patient. When he went out the front door, he found the messenger boy sitting on the front steps.

"Is Miss Opie going to get well?" asked Martin, his big brown eyes pensive.

"In time," said Doc.

"My mamma says you're the best doctor in the whole territory." The boy made an expansive gesture with his hands.
"Mamma says you can make Miss Opie well."

"I'll do my best."

"What are you going to do now?"

"A whole lot of thinking."

Martin rubbed his nose and grinned at Doc. "Your pantlegs
are sure gonna get dirty."

Doc smiled. "This time I'm going to think while I walk, not
on my knees."

"I'll bet your mamma will be glad," nodded the boy. "Does
she spank you when you get your pants dirty?"

"Not anymore," said Doc as he moved off along the street.
"She used to, though."

Martin's face broke into an understanding grin as Doc
walked away.

Doc went over to the jail. He wanted to talk to Frank Kimbrough. The young man's stricken face haunted him. Remembering when he had been locked up in that same cell, Doc
knew how deserted Frank must feel. Some inner compulsion
moved Doc to pity for Frank. Even though the prisoner had
evidently killed Jim, he was still a troubled fellow human
being. What was it Amos had said about Doc? That he'd spo-
ken like Jim Balinte used to talk? Opie had asked if he wanted
the job of replacing the dead philosopher.

Yes, Doc told himself. *I want the job. As soon as the killer's
stopped.*

Stepping inside the jail office, Doc saw Sid Harris sitting at
the desk.

"Hello, Doc." Sid looked up from the newspaper he was
reading.

"Hello, Sid. Where's Amos?"

"He said he had to go see a lady. Don't think he'll be gone
long. What can I do for you?"

Doc pushed a thumb towards the cell area. "Frank done any
talking yet?"

"Not so's you'd notice. He's been sitting on his bunk brooding ever since I came on duty." Sid folded his newspaper. "He hasn't got much to say."

"Let me in the cell, Sid. I want to talk to him."

"You can give it a try. Don't know as you'll have any luck."

Sid took the key ring off a peg on the wall, led the way back to the cell block, and inserted the massive key in the lock.

"You got a visitor, Frank."

Doc entered the cell. Sid locked the door behind him and went back to the front office. Doc sat down on the bunk beside Frank.

"I didn't do it," said Frank. The intensity of his voice reminded Doc of his own feelings when he'd been in Frank's place.

"Frank," Doc said in an earnest but reasonable tone, "how do you account for the fact that we found your boot heel marks in three different places where crimes had been committed?"

"What makes you so sure they were my tracks?"

"Like we told you before," Doc said patiently, "your right boot heel is worn down. It makes a very distinctive mark."

"I can't help it if my heel wears down like that. It always does. It's the way I walk that make it wear." Frank appealed for help. "Couldn't somebody else have a worn-down heel, too?"

"It's not likely someone else's heel would be worn down in exactly the same way. Your tracks match the prints Amos and I found when Jim was killed."

"I tell you I didn't kill him!" Frank shouted. "You've got to believe me! Those couldn't have been my tracks!"

"Then where were you when Jim was killed?"

Frank slumped wearily down on the bunk. He'd plainly given up hope that anyone would believe him. "I already told you. I was out back in the livery barn mucking out the horse stalls. The last time I saw Jim, he was alive and walking out the front door of the stable."

"All right, Frank. Let's assume that you didn't kill Jim." Frank's eyes lit up as Doc continued. "Where were you when Bill got bushwhacked?"

"Same place. That's a big livery barn. It takes me several hours to clean the whole place out. I didn't shoot Bill. I wouldn't go off and leave my job when I'm supposed to be on duty. When Mr. Collins goes off for the night and leaves me in charge I pay attention to business. He's been too good to me for me to ever let him down like that."

Something clicked in the back of Doc's memory. It was something to do with the relationship between Bryce and Frank. Doc worried it around in his head for a bit, but the association wouldn't come clear.

"One more question, Frank. Did you fire a shot at me through the front window of my house a few nights back?"

"No, sir. I never did." Frank's voice was emphatic.

"I found your tracks in the vacant lot across from my house the next morning," said Doc. "Jim was with me. He thought he knew who the tracks belonged to. He was going to double-check and let me know. Then he got killed. That's one of the reasons why I thought you might have killed him."

"All I can tell you is that I didn't kill Jim."

Doc didn't know what else to say. The two men sat on the bunk and stared moodily at the wall on the other side of the cell. A large horsefly crawled up the wall, launched itself into flight, and buzzed noisily out the window.

Frank broke the uneasy silence. "Dr. Killian, when the sheriff arrested me, you said something that's been worrying me more than anything else. You asked if I'd killed your wife. Why in the world did you ask that?"

"I haven't been able to find out who killed her."

"It couldn't have been me because I was standing at the side of Mr. Noel's house smoking a cigar when you found your wife. I heard you give this big yell and started to go inside. Just about that time Mr. Collins came around the corner. He and I went in together. You can ask him if that isn't the truth."

"What were you doing outside Noel's house that night?"

"I was listening to the music. Things were slow at the stable. Mr. Collins had told me it would be all right if I came over for a while and looked in on the party. That's one of the reasons I like Mr. Collins. He's always doing something nice for me."

An alarm bell sounded inside Doc's head. Slowly the gears of his memory meshed and then speeded up until he suddenly had the answer to a lot of questions. A simple explanation for such a complex chain of events.

He jumped up and shouted. "Hey, Sid! Open up!"

Instead of Sid, Amos opened the cell door. "Frank tell you something?"

"Yes, he did," said Doc. "I think I know the killer."

Amos' mouth dropped open. "You sure?"

"Pretty damned sure. But I need your help to wind this up."

"Anything you say, Doc." Amos slammed and locked the cell door. "Who did it?"

"Can't tell you yet." Doc hurried out to the office. "Could you round up Big Bill, Bryce, and especially Bob? I want all four of you over to my place for a poker game."

"You mean now?" spluttered Amos. "This afternoon? What kind of game are you playing?"

"Poker. Five-card draw," said Doc. "Special game in memory of Jim. Never mind why. You just get the other players."

"What the hell's the use of playing cards this time of day? If you're so damned sure about the killer, why don't you let me arrest him?"

"I'm not that sure, Amos. Couple things I got to check out first. I figure my best chance is to get you all together in one room. Depending on how the others act, I'll be able to make my decision. Will you do it my way?"

Amos nodded. "O.K. I'll play along for one more hand. What you want me to do about Frank?"

"Leave him where he is for right now," said Doc. "He'll be safe here."

Amos scratched his head. "You mean it wouldn't be safe to turn him loose?"

"That's right. Frank knows more than he thinks he does about all this. I don't want him out in town talking."

Amos turned to his deputy. "Sid, keep Frank locked up and

don't let anybody in to talk with him until I get back. C'mon, Doc. Let's get that poker game started."

When Doc got home he went to the kitchen and set up the poker table. He pulled six chairs around, put out a deck of cards and very carefully arranged six stacks of chips close to the edge of the table at each place. Then he settled down to wait.

Which one is it going to be? Amos is in the clear. Big Bill's just window dressing. Got to be either Bob or Bryce. But which? If my little scheme works I'll know soon enough. Then what? Guess I'll just have to let Amos make the arrest. Sure be glad when this game's over.

The front door banged open and Amos came stomping into the kitchen. He glanced at Doc, took in the poker setup, and sat down on Doc's right. "Ready to tell me who you think it is?"

"Not yet, Amos. You'll know pretty soon. Find all the players?"

"Yeh. Got Bill out of bed. He's still not very strong, but said he'd come along. Bryce was at the stable. Bob had to finish with a customer. They'll all be here soon."

Doc offered the sheriff a cigar. They both lit up. "While we're waiting, Amos, tell me what you found out about the woman Bryce said he was visiting the night Bill got shot."

"How in hell'd you know I was checking her out?"

Doc smiled. "When I went over to see Frank, Sid said you were out seeing a woman."

"I saw her. Said Bryce was with her that night. Couldn't remember the exact time he was there. Seemed flustered I knew about her and Bryce. Asked me not to tell her husband. Told her I wouldn't."

Doc puffed on his cigar. "Right gentlemanly of you. Wouldn't want to cause Bryce trouble with an irate husband, would you?"

"That wasn't the reason I promised her not to tell." Amos studied the ash on his stogie. "We kinda made a deal. Me to keep my mouth shut, her to give information."

"About what?" Doc leaned forward in his chair.

Amos' ears glowed red. "Don't quite know how to tell you this, but the woman said some prominent businessman in town was known to be carrying a torch for your wife right up to the time she was killed. Said she didn't know who the man was. Heard it thirdhand on the gossip line."

Prominent businessman? Who was the most prosperous man in Gila Crossing? Bob Noel! Little worms of jealousy gnawed at Doc's brain. Was Noel the man Jeanne had been involved with before she met him? That smooth-talking banker and his out-of-town witness! Maybe Dave Burns had been coached about what to say when they met. Noel had better play a mighty careful hand when the game started.

There came a pounding on the front door. Amos went to answer. Bill, Bryce, and Bob came in. They all looked a little puzzled about the sudden poker invitation.

Doc didn't try to play the gracious host. "Sit down," he said. "Let's play cards."

Chapter 19

"Is this your idea of a joke?" snorted Bob.

"No joke," said Doc.

Bob consulted his watch. "I have an important meeting in just one hour."

"This game won't last very long," said Doc.

"I don't usually play cards in the middle of the afternoon." Bryce hitched his pants up. "Can't this game wait until tonight?"

"Afraid not." Doc riffled the cards.

Bill looked gaunt and shaky. "What's this all about, Doc? I'm still not in very good shape. Shouldn't really be out of bed yet."

"You'll find out soon enough," said Doc. "Sit down. All of you."

Bill sat down at Doc's left. Amos on his right. "You sit next to Bill, Bryce," said Doc. "Bob, sit next to Amos." The empty sixth chair was opposite Doc.

He began to shuffle. An awkward silence held the group. "Uh—Doc," stammered Amos, "you expecting anyone else?"

"Nope. Just the five of us."

"Then who's the sixth chair for?"

Doc kept flipping cards. "In memory of Jim." He finished dealing. "O.K., let's ante up. We're using chips today. Bryce, why don't you divvy up the chips at Jim's chair? Give Bob half and you keep the rest."

Bryce and Bob gave Doc a baffled look, looked at each other, shrugged and divided the chips.

"I'll open," said Bill. He threw in one counter.

Everybody stayed. The pot grew.

"Who needs cards?" asked Doc.

"Two for me," Bill growled.

Bryce drummed his fingers on the table. "Two."

"I'll stand pat." Bob closed his hand.

"Gimme one," from Amos.

Doc took two.

"Since we're playing for chips," Bill boomed, "I'll raise three."

Bryce threw in his chips. "Must have got him a couple deuces."

Bob laid his hand down and added to the pot.

"Can't make it on this hand." said Amos. "I fold." .

Doc put three chips out. "What you got?"

The four remaining players fanned their cards out. Bob won the pot with a full house.

Bob raked in his winnings. "What we doing here, Doc?"

"Playing cards." Doc gathered up the pasteboards and handed the deck to Bill. "Your deal."

"C'mon, cut the crap," said Bob. "I've got other things to do besides play cards in the middle of the afternoon."

Bill laid the cards down. All eyes were on Doc. He hitched his chair up a little closer to the table. Smoke curled upwards from his cigar as he regarded the other players.

"I've got something important to tell you." He coughed. "Throat seems a mite dry. Better get me a drink."

Doc started to stand up. As he rose his thighs caught the table, tipped it, causing cards and chips to slide off. "Oh, Christ! What a clumsy idiot I am. Help me pick this mess up."

The five men got down on their hands and knees crawling around picking things up. Doc circled around helping first one and then the other all the time muttering his apologies. Soon cards, chips, and men, were all back in their usual order.

"All right, Doc. You're not that clumsy," fumed Bob. "What's this all about? What are you up to?"

"Solving several crimes," said Doc grimly. "I may as well

start at the beginning. On the night Jeanne was killed, all of
you were out of the ballroom at that same time. Ever since
then I've had the feeling that one of you might have killed
her."

Jaws dropped. The other men stirred uneasily in their chairs.
Quick glances swept around the circle. Doc stared steadily at
Bob.

"Jeanne's killing was so senseless," Doc bored in, "I tried to
find some connection from her past that might explain her
death. The only explanation I could come up with was that
she'd broken off a love affair when she met me and the disgrun-
tled lover finally killed her. No one in Gila Crossing could tell
me who the man was. Amos learned today that he was a prominent businessman. You're the richest man in town, Bob."

The banker nervously fiddled with his diamond stickpin. His
hard eyes never left Doc's face. "It wasn't me. I've been married to Ruth for twenty-five years. Never strayed off the reser-
vation."

Doc raised a restraining hand. "After I came back from
Yuma, I started having trouble with some boot tracks. Seems
like every place I went, those tracks went with me. They were
outside the schoolhouse window one afternoon when I was
talking to Opie. Somebody took a shot at me one night. The
next day I found those same prints across the street from my
house. Jim helped me look at those tracks. He thought he knew
who made them. Jim was murdered before he could tell me
what he knew. While he was dying he tried to leave me a message."

"One of the few things I've missed hearing," said Bob. "What
was the message?"

"Three words, written in blood, on the backside of Bill's
anvil," said Doc. "Middle word was illegible. Other two were
'think' and 'track.' Didn't mean anything to me at the time.
When Bill got bushwhacked, I found the tracks again. They
were all around Jim's place the day he was killed. When the
bell tower fell on me and Opie, the tracks showed up there the

next morning. Me and Amos set out to find out who made the tracks."

Doc cleared his throat. "We met Frank going home from work. Then I knew what Jim's message meant. What he tried to write was 'think Frank tracks.' Even in his dying moments he didn't want to accuse anyone unjustly, so he used the word 'think.'"

"Frank's boots were making the tracks," cut in Amos. "I arrested him. He claimed he wasn't the killer. I'm still not convinced."

"Let me finish my story, Amos," said Doc. "I went back to the jail and talked with Frank today. He denied killing Jeanne and Jim. Said he was standing outside Noel's house on the night Jeanne died. Then I thought I knew who had really made the tracks. But I had to check my theory."

"You mean to tell us," flared Bryce, "that you're basing your accusations of who killed Jeanne and Jim on some footprints?"

"They were very special prints, Bryce. Frank's right heel was worn down in a certain way. He walks with a peculiar gait that causes him to drag his right foot. That's not his regular walk. He just imitates somebody."

Amos grabbed Doc's arm. "Who does Frank mimic?"

"That's what I found out while we were all crawling around on the floor. I found another worn-down heel. It's your heel, Bryce!"

"You're crazy!" screamed Bryce. "I couldn't have killed Jeanne. Opie told you she saw me standing outside Noel's house that night when it happened."

"It wasn't you she saw," Doc's eyes blazed. "Frank looks and acts so much like you it fooled Opie from a distance. You killed Jeanne!"

Bryce jumped up and pulled his gun. "It was an accident! I didn't mean to kill her! That night in the library I was going to make her run away with me."

Doc regarded his enemy. Here before him was the man who had killed his wife and his best friend. This man had also shot another friend and tried to kill him on at least two different occasions. Because of this man Opie lay in bed with a broken leg. And yet, to all outward appearances, the man before him was the same old Bryce he had known for a long time.

"Now you know, Doc. It was Jeanne I was in love with. Before you came to town I had her all to myself. I even thought I was going to marry her. She was the first woman I ever seriously proposed to. But after you came around it all changed. After Jeanne met you she told me our romance was over, that she had never really cared enough for me to consider marrying me." Bryce glared at Doc out of bloodshot eyes.

"Even after you got married, I kept after her. Whenever we'd meet I'd tell her about how much I still loved her. She wouldn't have anything to do with me. Told me she loved you and to quit bothering her. It was a low blow to my ego. Evidently she recognized me for what I am—an empty shell." Bryce lowered his eyes and his voice.

"Maybe it doesn't mean anything to you, but I've never had anything in my whole life. Nothing I ever really valued. Nothing I ever really wanted. None of the good times, or women, or business success meant anything to me. It wasn't until I met Jeanne that I finally found something that had some value to me." Bryce's voice shook with emotion.

"I didn't give up hope. I kept trying to get her to change her mind. She had a will of iron. The more I hounded her the more obstinate she became. She was always kind to me. Jeanne never blew up and insulted me like some women would have done. No, she just steadfastly refused to have anything to do with me. She told me, time and time again, that I was not the man for her, that she had you. That I should go find another woman to marry. This just made me want her more." The gun in Bryce's hand wavered. He had a bad case of nerves.

"That night at the party I had been dancing with Jeanne. Her nearness and beauty about drove me out of my mind. I lured her into the library by telling her I had something very important to tell her about you. I lied to you about that. She didn't go there to find a book of poetry. You had already given her all the poetry she'd ever need."

Bryce's hand shook, but he steadied the gun. "When we got there I lost control. Told her I still loved her. That I couldn't abide the thought of her being married to another man. I was insane with passion and jealousy. I told her I was going to make her go away with me right that moment. I was going to kidnap her. She tried to calm me down with words. They didn't work. I grabbed her by the arm and started to pull her out of the room. That's when she pulled the gun."

It was hard for Bryce to go on. His jaw muscles twitched as he forced himself to continue his confession. "She must have known I might pull some crazy stunt like that on the night of the party. She had come prepared to prove that she preferred you over me. I tried to take the gun away from her. In the struggle it got turned around and went off. I never meant to kill her! You've got to believe that! I really did love her."

At last Doc knew exactly how his wife had died. It was no comfort to him to hear the details.

"So you let them convict me and send me to Yuma." Doc said it as a statement and not as a question.

Bryce had the grace to drop his eyes. "Yes." His reply was barely audible. "I was a coward as well as a murderer. I framed you just as though I had made formal charges against you. I framed you by my silence. But, Doc," he looked up, his eyes begging for understanding, "you've got to understand that I wasn't in my right mind."

Doc struggled to accept Bryce's reasoning. It is always difficult to listen to the side of a story that you don't want to believe.

Bryce's voice droned on. "The shock of killing Jeanne, my hatred for you, these things caused me to keep silent. I had killed the woman we both loved and sent an innocent man to prison. It wasn't until after they sent you to Yuma that I fully realized what I had done. Since then I haven't known a moment's peace. I try to sleep at night, but my dreams keep waking me up. It's always the same dream. First the look in

Jeanne's eyes as she fell and then the look in your eyes when the judge passed sentence. I have not been a man since the day you left town. I've been a cowardly, ashamed, disgraced, hunted animal.

"And all the time I knew that someday you would come back and find me." Bryce looked at Doc with haunted eyes. "I never doubted that you would eventully learn the truth. But, coward that I am, I tried to make it as difficult as possible for you."

Doc spoke up. "Like filing down a buggy linchpin?"

"It was easy." Bryce gave a flicker of a smile. "When I got the buggy from Bill's shop that day you took Opie for a ride I just switched pins. I had an old one laying around the stable that had been pretty well worn down and been replaced. I gave it a few more licks with a file and put it back on your buggy."

"What did you learn from eavesdropping when Opie and I were talking at the schoolhouse?" Doc prompted.

"Nothing much," Bryce shrugged, "except Opie gave me an alibi. When she told you she had been watching me through the window on the night of the Noels' party I realized it was Frank she had seen. It was a bit of luck for me to help throw you off my track. But I didn't want to take a chance on you finding it had really been Frank that Opie saw instead of me."

"Is that the reason you took a shot at me through my front window?"

"Yes." Bryce took a step backward and warily eyed Amos who had made a move for his own gun. "It was a dumb thing to do. I should have brought a rifle instead of a handgun. I never was a good pistol shot."

"You came pretty damned close. I could feel the breeze when that slug went past my head," Doc went on relentlessly. "Why did you kill Jim?"

"For the same reason I had been trying to kill you. To keep him quiet. I knew he had figured out where the heel prints had come from. Or at least he thought he had. I noticed Jim walking up and down the street looking at tracks. He followed them into the blacksmith shop where I had gone to talk to Bill, and then he came over to the livery stable. He walked out back in my stable and said hello to Frank. Then he came up front to see me."

Bryce edged another step over towards the front door. "I asked him what he was doing and he told me he had followed Frank's tracks to there. He said he couldn't believe Frank had taken a shot at you. Then he left to go back over to the forge and double-check the trail he had been following. That's when I ran over to the saloon and got a drifter to come over and tell Frank about a wagon being broke down at the crossing with a pregnant woman in it. I gave the drifter a dollar and told him he'd find Frank out back and not to bother talking to anyone else. I wanted to get Bill out of town so I could catch Jim in the blacksmith shop alone and kill him."

Doc started to move towards Bryce. Bryce waved him back with the gun and stepped up closer to the table. "I didn't know how much Jim had told Bill so I decided I'd have to kill him too. I hurried back to my office and saw the drifter going out back to give the message to Frank. Frank left and delivered the message to Bill. Bill lit right out for the river. Frank came back and went to work again. I was just getting ready to go over to the blacksmith shop when Jim came into my office again. He said he'd double-checked Frank's tracks and wanted me to come look at them to make sure he was right about them. I told him I had an important engagement and couldn't go with him."

Bryce eyed the spectators grimly. "Jim and I left about the same time. He said he was going to go down and get the sheriff to pull Frank in for questioning. I pretended like I was going the other way. But I doubled back behind the buildings and found Jim inside the blacksmith shop. He had stopped on his way to the jail to take one more look at the tracks. He was a very cautious man."

"Not cautious enough," Doc remarked dryly.

"No," said Bryce. "I slipped up behind him and cut him with a knife. He never knew what hit him. I left him laying there and took out after Bill. The forge was closed up and I didn't figure anyone would find Jim before I got back. I took a short cut down to the river and got across to the other side and set up my bushwhack before Bill got there. He was like a sitting duck. Any ordinary man would have died when my bullet hit him. That's just another sample of how my luck's been running lately."

Bill grunted and started to move. Bryce shook the gun at him and motioned for him to sit still. "I didn't wait to see if Bill was dead. I had to get back to town and get rid of Jim's body. I didn't want it found so close to my place of business. When I got back to town it was pretty quiet. I pulled Jim's body out the back door and drug it up to the funeral parlor. When I got inside with the body I was feeling pretty cocky, so I put Jim in the display case up in the front window. Don't know what made me do it. Some sense of showing off, or something. Like I've already said, I haven't been thinking too good lately."

"I don't know about that," Doc said between clenched teeth. "Pushing the bell tower over was a pretty good idea. At least people might have thought that was a real accident."

Bryce gave a sheepish half grin. "In a way, I suppose that would have seemed like an accident. Everybody in town has known for years that the tower was about to fall down by itself. When you and Opie left the auction I waited a minute and then eased outside and pushed it over."

Amos spoke for the first time. "What do you think you're going to do now, Bryce?"

"I've got a fast horse outside. Best race horse from my stable. I'm just going to walk out of here and head for the border. Anybody that tries to stop me is going to get a belly full of lead." Bryce started inching his way towards the door.

Doc lunged for the gun. Big Bill lifted the table and flung it towards Bryce. At the same moment Amos pulled his gun and fired. Bryce went down under the impact of the table and the bullet. Doc sprawled on top of the table.

Blood oozed out of Bryce's nose and mouth. Amos' bullet had passed through his lungs. Big Bill pulled the table away.

Doc grabbed a kitchen towel and tried to stanch the bleeding. Bryce coughed up more blood. Doc cradled Bryce in his arms.

The light started fading from Bryce's gray-green eyes. He looked up. "I'm sorry, Doc." Then he died.

Doc laid Bryce's body down. He looked at the others. "He was once my friend." Doc sadly shook his head. "When I was at Yuma I used to dream of this moment. Revenge has a bitter taste."

Amos pulled Doc to his feet. "Give me a hand, Bill. Let's get Bryce out of here." They picked the body up, carried it out the door.

Bob touched Doc's shoulder. "Satisfied about me now?"

"Owe you an apology." Doc held out his hand.

Bob shook it. "None needed. What you aim to do now?"

Doc sighed, took a long breath, and squared his shoulders. "Go courting. I'm going to see if I can win Opie back."

Chapter 20

After Bob left, Doc hurriedly slicked up and changed into his best clothes. He left the house cutting kitty-corner across vacant lots to the next street. Noel's house was in front of him. Doc went around to the backyard and found a rosebush. Ruth Noel had painstakingly watered and cultivated the plant to make it grow in the arid climate. Doc never hesitated. He stole an armful of roses.

Off he went to Opie's house. He knocked on the front door. Mrs. Mognette answered.

"My goodness, Doctor," she gasped, "where did you get those roses?"

"I found them growing on a rose tree."

Mrs. Mognette smiled and looked archly at Doc. "Are you going to a wedding or a funeral, all dressed up like that?"

"My wedding, I hope."

"Are you going to invite me to your wedding, Doctor?"

"My dear lady, you'll be among the first to know when it's held. And now, if you'll excuse me, I want to see Opie. In private, if you don't mind. It might not be a bad idea if you went for a walk. I'll take care of Miss Opie." He stepped through the open door.

Mrs. Mognette went outside, turned for one last question. "And who might you be going to marry?"

"Three guesses," said Doc as he closed the door. He went upstairs to Opie's bedroom. The door was closed. He knocked. There was no answer. He knocked again.

"The door's unlocked," Opie said. "Come in."

Doc entered the room. Opie lay on the bed as before except

that she had been propped up to a sitting position with several pillows behind her back. She looked at Doc with surprise. "I don't believe we've met."

Doc removed his hat and gave a sweeping bow. "Allow me to introduce myself, madam. My name is Killian. V. E. Killian. I'm a philosopher by vocation, a medicine man by avocation."

"Interesting," admitted Opie.

"I'm also a thief," said Doc glancing at the roses.

"Even more interesting," Opie's eyes sparkled.

"Not professionally, you understand." Doc held the flowers out to her. "It's just a hobby of mine, this stealing. I don't really spend much time at it."

"I see," said Opie taking the flowers. She pressed her face to them and inhaled their fragrant aroma.

"A curious person might want to know where my latest crime took place." Doc held his hat over his heart.

"I'm curious," Opie nodded.

"In the backyard of banker Noel's house. In broad daylight." Doc gave a little swagger. "Not too many thieves operate in such a grand manner."

"I should hope not," replied Opie starting to smile. "Won't Mrs. Noel be mad?"

"A little bit at first. Later on, after Mrs. Noel learns of the romantic purpose of the theft, she will be very forgiving."

Opie's smile faded. "Am I to consider these flowers as a romantic offering?"

"Why, yes. Flowers for the fair. A rose by any other name. My love is like a red, red rose. Flowers are merely nature's way of reflecting the beauty of her fairest daughter, Opie." He bowed again.

"Are you drunk?"

Doc gravely considered his hat. "Not at the moment, madam. At least not drunk on spirits. A little drunk perhaps with the spirit of a new beginning, a new leaf turned in the book of life. But not drunk to the extent of not knowing what I'm doing."

"What are you doing?" Opie's blue eyes bored into him.

"Trying to tell you that I've been a damned fool. In more ways than one."

"I knew you were in one way." Opie cocked her head to one side. "What's the other way?"

"It took me a long time to figure out that Bryce had killed Jeanne and Jim."

Opie was instantly alert. "But how? I saw him through the window the night of the party when Jeanne was killed."

"You thought you saw him. What you really saw was Frank. They looked so much alike from a distance that it had you fooled."

"How do you know he killed Jeanne?"

"He told me so."

"And Jim?"

"He admitted that, also."

Opie frowned. "Why?"

"An accident with Jeanne. To keep Jim from talking."

"Where's Bryce now?"

"Dead."

"How?"

Doc's voice lowered. "He pulled a gun on a bunch of us. He was going to run away. Amos shot him."

Opie's eyes clouded. "I'm sorry."

"So am I," said Doc. "And yet, it solves many problems."

"For instance?" asked Opie.

Doc pulled up a chair and sat down at Opie's bedside. He looked deep into her eyes. "Now I can start living again."

"Good for you."

"I mean that," said Doc. "I realize now that what you told me about life being for the living is the truth. I haven't been living for the past three years. I've been existing. I was so wrapped up in my own petty world that I didn't give any thought to other people. Nothing mattered to me except my search for Jeanne's killer. Now that the mystery is solved I'm ready to rejoin the human race."

"What about Jeanne?" Opie's voice went up a notch.

"She's gone," Doc shrugged. "When she died a part of me died with her. What's left of me is ready to go on and make a new life. I'll always love the memory of the short bit of life I shared with Jeanne. But reality is that she no longer exists—except in my memory."

Opie looked at him intently. "What do you intend to do now?"

"Get married again."

"Oh," said Opie. "Anyone in particular?"

"You."

"Don't believe I'm interested." Opie yawned and patted her mouth.

"But you've got to be!" Doc's brow furrowed. "There's no one else for me."

"You'll find somebody if you keep looking."

"I've already looked all I intend to look," said Doc gruffly. "You're the one for me. Why do you have to be so contrary all of a sudden?"

"You mean you liked me better when I was chasing you?"

"Frankly, yes," said Doc. "At least then I knew where I stood. How come now that I've finally come to my senses and want to marry you, you turn skittish on me?"

"Turn about's fair play. Why should I marry you?" asked Opie.

"Because I want you."

"Who cares about your wants?"

"But, Opie. I need you."

"Who cares what you need?"

"But, Opie, I can't live without you."

"That's your problem."

"But—Opie—I love you!"

"Why didn't you say so? Are you ever going to kiss me?"

Doc did. Fervently. With great care and tenderness. Not once. Not twice. But three times running with only the briefest of pauses in between kisses for a short breath of air.

Doc and Opie clung to each other for a long time. Finally Opie pushed him off to arm's length. "Tell me something."

"Anything."

"What's your first name, pardner?"

Doc threw back his head and roared with laughter. "I thought you knew."

"No. That's one of the few things about you I don't know."

"It's Victor," said Doc.

"I believe you are," said Opie as she pulled Doc back down beside her.